Desire

By

J.C. Aaron

Copyright © 2023 by – J.C. Aaron – All Rights Reserved.

It is not legal to reproduce, duplicate, or transmit any part of this document in either electronic means or printed format. Recording of this publication is strictly prohibited.

Table of Contents

Dedication	i
Acknowledgements	ii
About the Author	iii
Prologue	1
Desire.	4
II	7
III	13
IV	19
V	25
Part II	31
I	32
II	33
III	39
IV	44
V	49
VI	52
VII	56
VIII	60
Part III	63
I	64
II	67
III	69
IV	72
V	75

VI	79
VII	81
VIII	85
IX	90
X	94
XI	96
XII	99
XIII	104
XIV	110
Part IV	113
I	114
II	119
III	121
IV	125
V	131
VI	136
VII	143
VIII	148
Epilogue	155

Dedication

To Richard O'Hara, the best English teacher, a good friend and the first person I shared my writing with. Thanks for keeping it real.

Acknowledgements

Mom, Dad, Grandma Cicio, Grandma Torres, Grandpa Fuster, my 8 beautiful siblings: Xiomara, Kayla, Ava, Kennedy, Liana, Allison, Joey, Johnny, as well as all my aunts, uncles, and cousins. You are such amazing people in my life! My friends Spencer, Dorcas, Howard and the Zevin family, Dov and family, The Horton Family, The Panagia family, The May family, Jaye and the family at TIM, my yoga friends Chris, Andy, Svitri and Cate. Tom, Nevin and the Book Club in Barcelona, the IBEW, and all those I've known who have passed on before seeing this book being published, you are my guardian angels.

About the Author

J.C. Aaron, a New Jersey native, writes cathartic stories that inspire, uplift and entertain others. When he is not writing, he enjoys nature walks, music concerts and quality time with family and friends. He lives in Springfield, NJ.

Disclaimer:

This story is a fictional narrative and any relationship between person, place, or things is completely coincidental. And I don't claim any injury or cause by anybody reading this novella.

Prologue

"To the pure all is pure."

- Anonymous

Thursday July 4th, 2013

"The two brothers worked out a deal!" Zechariah Von Barstool shouted to his mob full of self-righteous missionaries each armed with pitchforks and torches marching their way to Alistor Street to burn down Xavier's home.

"We're burning it down!"

"Yeah, burn it down!"

Malinda sat in her rocking chair, crying with her eyes closed. She heard shouting at the front door. She moved the sofa earlier to act as a barrier although the size of this crowd would stampede right in. Glimmers of light shone through the boarded up windows, depicting her inner struggle. She opened her eyes, looked up at the ceiling and pleaded, "Almighty God, please forgive us for our sins."

As she prayed the front door burst open by a battering ram and the mob flooded the premises. Malinda looked at the leader Zechariah, whose face was battered and covered in dirt. She immediately passed out from fear. "Leave her inside, she'll be happier this way!" Zechariah screamed as his men began setting the house ablaze. And the rest of his mob filled the streets outside, blocking all roads from oncoming emergency personnel vehicles.

Meanwhile, Selah Rosado stood away from the crowd, hidden within the shadows of Alistor Street. She watched as Xavier's house burst into flames. She cried knowing that Xavier's wife, Malinda, was dying inside.

Selah turned to look away but jumped upon noticing a man standing directly behind her. "So what'd you see?" He was so close she smelled the menthol cigarettes coming off his breath. "I'm an undercover cop." She couldn't see his face amidst the thickness of the smoke, but she noticed his badge drawn, glistening in the dark. She thought about the gun in her purse, it was unregistered and had its barcode etched off. Then the man said, "I'll ask you again. So what'd you see? You can either talk here or at the Tri-City precinct."

"It was horrible…" She coughed before making the decision to run as fast as she could. The cop tugged at her purse strap and broke it off and the purse fell to the pavement; but Selah kept running. He watched her and pulled out his radio to page the precinct, "I have a witness on the move down Alistor Street, heading towards Roselle. I'll cut her off on 5th Ave."

Selah ran down the nearest alley, out of sight. She looked back and saw no one chasing her. She continued for ten blocks and noticed every house light off. And after ten minutes of sprinting, she hid behind a bush outside of a homemade ice cream parlor to catch her breath. She looked into the window of the ice cream shop and noticed a white reflection coming off the freezers like a ghostly apparition. She was about to stand up, when a black Cadillac zoomed past at 100 miles per hour.

After that the coast was clear. She got up and ran, this time telling herself she wouldn't stop; she'd make it home, grab her car and skip town. Now was her chance while the city was in upheaval. She scaled up her driveway on 5th Ave and jumped into her sedan and turned on the engine. "That's not a good idea." The undercover cop said, sitting in the backseat.

"How the heck did you get here so quickly?" She snapped, looking through the rearview mirror into his dark eyes. He looked handsome, with a thin clean shaven face and stylish hair, reminding her of John Stamos. Too bad her heart was taken already.

"I assume you'll want this back." He handed her her purse with the broken strap. She grabbed it and clutched it to her breast. "So are you gonna talk?" He asked.

"You don't understand!" She began sobbing. "I miss him so much!"

Desire.

Ever since I was a boy I've desired to be rich and live an extravagant lifestyle. And that was a lofty desire for someone like me who grew up in the Tri-Cities, the place where someone would kill you for a bite to eat, the place where you were told that you get what you deserve. I've had countless setbacks throughout the years but I've only grown more persistent because deep down in my heart I knew I'd never be satisfied until I had the freedom to do what I wanted to do when I wanted to do it. But it all started with a burning desire.

As a kid I grew up with my older brother Marshall, a misfit, who at the age of seven got suspended from St. Mary's for smoking cigarettes in the bathroom, then, a few years later, he got expelled for tying up Sister Clarissa and locking her in the office to ask her about sex, drugs and rock and roll.

I was always fascinated how Marshall weaseled his way out of everything, like when he got in trouble for throwing up gang signs to police at age eleven and our mother enabled him by laughing it off and saying, "it's the police who were rotten for not letting kids have fun anymore!" All my mother wanted was for Marshall and I to be successful and make a lot of money. And Marshall, my role model, made money unconventionally. After he was expelled from school he began working full time on the streets. He found a great scheme, hiding in the locker room of the Springlawn Country Club where he'd watch rich clientele store their Rolexes and Diamond rings in personalized safes; he'd memorize their codes, then steal the contents while they were out on a round of golf. "Payday!" Marshall announced upon entering our small one bedroom apartment in the Sticks (the worst neighborhood in the Tri-Cities). And there I was on the couch (really my bed) watching him for years come in and out at all hours of the night, jealous of how he never went to school and always had money. I, on the other hand, was three years younger than him, focused on school, and planned to get rich after ten more years of hard work (I had ambition to go to law school and be a lawyer). I remember those times well. I had straight A's and our mother had me already looking at colleges at 16. She said I would one day change the world and I believed her. My first milestone was the day I got accepted to UPenn.

But then I cracked under pressure, started failing my classes, which left me no choice but to run away from home and become a mercenary, following in Marshall's footsteps because he had moved out a few months prior to live on a mattress under the Cherry Street Bridge.

When I ran away all I had on me was my bicycle, twenty dollars in cash and a backpack with a twelve pack of beers, hoping that'd last the week. I didn't even make it all the way to the Cherry Street Bridge either because the bike tired me out, (never was much for athletics) so I slept on an abandoned train car for two nights until a transit cop pulled me up from a drunken stupor and checked me into a private inpatient facility; one of those shiny and clean on the outside type of places, while inside had quack docs, underpaid nurses, and bug problems.

I immediately outlined an escape plan to my first roommate Vince Libretti, who was interested, but he died the following night after the whole unit watched the original Nightmare on Elm Street; Vince was found in the basement, apparently, with his head stuck in the incinerator, but I didn't care, all I hoped was that my next roommate would be cool, someone who could match my great expectations. A real partner in crime.

And the following day while I was watching a soap, (okay... a Spanish novella), a nurse wheeled my next roommate into the room. I didn't even want to look over because the guy looked helpless and all bandaged up. Then, the nurse walked out and I heard the guy on the stretcher scream, "Don't come back here unless you get me more meds for the pain!" From the moment he spoke I knew it was my brother! Even though he was covered in bandages, I knew his voice from anybody. We were technically adopted brothers, but I always called him my blood. We were *two* misfits. "Marshall, you alright?" I asked.

"Of course brother. This place is a goldmine. I'm loaded. Why else would I be here? " He said, taking out a pill bottle from his pocket and shaking it to let me know it was full. I looked into his eyes which were dilated beyond capacity. At that moment I couldn't believe his fearlessness, nobody had zeal like Marshall.

"You mean you're not.."

"Ohh.. these bandages? Yeah they're for show."

II

I woke up from this dream in the middle of the night on a park bench just outside the Alamo in San Antonio, Texas. I didn't hear police sirens so I knew I was safe. For now.

Although I kept hearing eerie voices in my mind wherever I went.

"We see you X."

"X marks the dead man."

"We're waiting…"

Ever since I stole the diamonds I've been tormented by gruesome visions day and night. Yesterday, I saw a man with no chin standing in the street, saying, 'Xavier, don't you recognize me?" Then a bulldozer flattened him, squished his brains and pulverized his skeleton as the driver rolled his window down, tossed the cigarette from his mouth and sang Jungleland by Bruce Springsteen, 'Down…. in…. Jungle…..Land.'

I knew this was my karma for stealing the diamonds. And on top of that I was a wanted man. My picture was posted on every news station. And I had the opportunity to escape to Mexico after the robbery but I couldn't run without Selah, the love of my life.

I tried to go back to sleep but instead walked along the riverwalk hoping to figure out a plan. I waited 'til sunrise before stopping at a small cafe called Blissful Vibes to order a coffee and a muffin. I was immediately an eyesore; it must have been my ripped clothing and massive duffle bag slung over my shoulder; and I smelled awful after sleeping on a park bench the last two days. Sure enough after I ordered, the young woman at the counter kept staring at me. She finally excused herself to the kitchen where I heard her speaking discreetly over the phone. In panic, I fled out the back door and hitched the first bus out of the city, deciding the only sensible place would be to stop at my Uncle Charlie's cabin, way off the grid, deep in the bayou of Mississippi.

Uncle Charlie and my late Aunt Millie lived a two hour hike away from the nearest town of Fulton, Mississippi. And even after ten years I remembered the trail. Maybe it was muscle memory because Marshall and I used to come down here and stay every summer when we were kids and play among the vicious gators, poisonous frogs and monstrous snakes. And still to this day, at twenty nine years old, I caught myself looking for the Lochness monster in the bayou, remembering my Uncle Charlie telling Marshall and I the urban legend.

I found the cabin finally… hidden in the distance within the recesses of trees and shrubbery. Of course my uncle still had both the American and Confederate flag hanging from the front porch and the same two wooden rocking chairs, combined they had to be older than Melchizedek.

Ugh, I looked down at the splattering of mud and debris on my shoes and pants. Why'd I think to come out here? And the duffle bag felt heavier now, I couldn't wait to put it down. I hurried up to the front porch to bang on the door. Within seconds, my uncle opened the door pointing a long nose rifle out at me. I lowered my sunglasses, put my hands up and gulped, "Hey uncle, it's your nephew!" as his hunting rifle was a foot from my face; Uncle Charlie blinked his eyes a couple times and remained silent. I yelled thinking maybe he was deaf now, he had to be almost seventy-five, "It's me. Xavier! I need a place to rest for a few days!"

He recognized me and lowered his rifle. "Come on in you muskrat! You scared me senseless, nobody ever pays me a visit."

"You look good Unc." I said, disregarding his disheveled appearance (worse than mine) and debaucherous state of his home.

"Thanks X. Well I don't do much going out anymore. Especially with all the liberals taking over the towns.." He sighed, unapologetically. "It's mighty good to see you though nephew. How long's it been?"

"Ten years…" I replied, staring at my uncle who seemed to have on the same stained coveralls from ten years ago. I remembered the signature brown, green and red splotches and pathetic stitchwork. He looked like a character out of a crossbreed of Hills Have Eyes and Texas Chainsaw Massacre.

"Since Aunt Millie..." Uncle Charlie said in a debilitated voice, hanging his gun on the ledge of the parlor window, which looked like a prime vantage point to catch an intruder from a hundred yards away. "I know Millie was your Ma's sister and all," Charlie began, "but you're still family to me Mr. Bonaparte." He coughed, his breath smelt of dry spirits, possibly gin. "I heard you were in law school, how they treat ya?"

"I passed the BAR exam four years ago and I've been busy ever since thank God…. I bought a nice house, married a beautiful wife and settled down. But you know the old saying: change is the only constant."

Uncle Charlie scratched his head, not registering what I said. "This ain't no place for a city boy, you know that."

"I needed a change of scenery." I replied, it was partly truthful.

"Well if you're staying for a while you should know, plenty of folks have been looking for a decent law'er." Charlie sat down on the sofa pulled out a fat cigar and lit it. "It's a shame but the state police have gone strict. They taking the 'sip' right out of Mississippi. Everybody and their first cousin wife gettin' charged with drunk driving." He coughed a few times. I put my bag next to a small table near the front door.

"So where's your old lady Malinda? You don't take her on unexpected trips down to the bayou?" He asked, chewing on the cigar end.

I laughed, nervously. "Truthfully I don't think we ever had a decent marriage, her and I. You know she became the biggest pain in the ass five years ago, around the time I realized that the only hobby we shared was drinking." I imitated swigging a bottle. "If you saw the amount of vodka bottles and beer cans sprawled about our bedroom back home you'd collapse. It was a hazard to even get up and take a piss in the night. One morning I tripped and fell right on my damn face. See this gash." I pointed at an old cut on my left cheek. "Sliced on the edge of a compacted beer can."

"Damn nephew. You gotta take care of yourself, and leave that self-pity elsewhere."

"At this point I've had it with self-pity!" I said triumphantly.

Uncle Charlie scratched his crack, then put his hand in his mouth to whistle up the steps, calling down a skinny golden retriever. "Hey X, meet Prince. He's a handsome devil ain't he."

"Yeah he's got a nice demeanor." I said, although the dog looked emaciated. "How long have you had him?"

"Got Prince as a pup eight years ago. And he's been my only company… I still haven't completely mourned Millie. I don't think I ever will though to be honest."

I wanted to brush over that subject because Aunt Millie was my favorite aunt and I might have cried seeing him get depressed.

"Hey Unc, I have some money to compensate you if you can offer me a few days to board here."

"Aww shucks mister money bag." He chuckled, "You're a godsend. It's just nice to have some human interaction."

I saw water tearing up in his eyes. I was about to tear up too. It was a good time to excuse myself for a minute. "Mind if I use the bathroom?" I asked.

"Yeah of course. Up the stairs to the left."

I walked, creaking up the staircase, where each step was unlevel, and halfway up I almost lost my balance. But luckily, I held onto the banister for dear life.

I reached the landing, turned to my left and froze upon seeing a pale, ghostly figure blocking the bathroom door. Instinctively, I shielded my eyes not wanting to witness another one of those horrible visions. Then the pale figure said, "Leave immediately! You are in danger. Your uncle knows everything."

"Who are you?" I asked.

"Never mind that. You'll thank me later." It said before disappearing. At that point I was already on my knees recalibrating myself back to sanity.

"Hey X. You alright? I heard a loud thump." Uncle Charlie called up the steps.

"I tripped but I'm alright."

"Be careful. Last thing I need is you suing my ass." Charlie laughed.

III

I looked at my watch. 5:41 PM. If I leave now I'd have enough time to make it out of the bayou before dusk, since the trails are difficult to navigate at night. I rushed down the steps straight to the door, picked up my duffle bag, which weighed a ton and pulled on the door handle but it burned my hand. "AHHHH." I screamed as some sort of toxic chemical burned my palm. Meanwhile, Uncle Charlie walked into the living room with his rifle cocked back, and shot one of the floorboards in front of me.

"You ain't going anywhere's nephew." He said, throwing a copy of the Tri-City Gazelle on the sofa so I could see. The front headline said: **Alistor Street Suspect's Home Burnt Down. 1 Dead.** Along with a picture of *my house* on fire and a picture of *me* in a suit. I remembered that suit, it's the one I wore the day of the Anderson trial a year ago.

"Holy fuck!" I gasped.

"I had a feeling you'd show here." Uncle Charlie moved closer. "Sit down, there's a lot we need to catch up on." I sat against my will, feeling a heavy burden. "I find it odd you turn up 'cause I been thinkin' 'bout where'd you wind up! Every damn paper has your mug on the front page. You think a shaved head is gonna save you?" Uncle Charlie laughed, holding one hand over his belching stomach.

"How'd you get the paper, I thought you didn't go into town?"

"Yeah I got a little Peach, been deliverin' me food and the paper for the last seven years. She works the fruit market and brings me the daily leftovers." He had a lopsided smile. "Says she's 18 now. 'Bout time."

I stood up to test his will.

"Hold it!" Uncle Charlie butted me in the face with his gun, forcing me to sit again. "I've been reading about your little adventures for the past few weeks. Let's open that duffle bag and see what you got."

"Trust me uncle you don't want any part in this!"

"Bullshit!" He peered down the barrel. "Open the bag!" He jabbed me again. "You're lucky I don't kill you off. Don't mistake my kindness for weakness."

"Fine!" I conceded. "Take it all if I care!" I looked across the room and saw Prince, the Golden Retriever whimpering in the corner.

"You're a generous nephew." He said, keeping the gun pointed at me, and motioning toward the bag. "Get on the floor and put your hands on your head, you can't be trusted. It's a shame what you did to your brother in the end." He bent over, unzipped the bag and stared within, immediately mesmerized by the diamonds.

"The whole mission was a mistake." I retorted. "Those diamonds are cursed."

"You must be an idiot if you think I'll believe that," He laughed, keeping one hand on the gun, and reaching the other into the bag to grab the largest diamond and analyze its tetrahedral shape. He noticed the inscription: **A13**. Then his body froze and he was stuck in a hunched over position.

"Xavier..." He managed to say, trembling.

"What's wrong?" I asked.

"My.... chest... something's... not... right." He shook and his lips quivered. "Can't... Bre...."

Then his whole body went limp. He fell back, hit his head on the hardwood floor, and dropped the gun and the diamond. I lunged over, pumped his chest and attempted CPR. But it was too late already because his heart had stopped. Prince, seeing me over his master, eyed me up and studied me. I nervously reached to grab the gun on the floor but Prince darted out and dug his teeth deep into my forearm. "You cunt!" I screamed and kneed the fucker in the abdomen. I must have broken one of his flimsy bones because I heard him let off a wail that sounded so agonizing (I still hear that sound to this day). There Prince laid debilitated on his side, and that's where I left him because I needed to escape. Dusk was approaching.

I made the sign of the cross over Uncle Charlie's body then grabbed the duffle bag of diamonds, jumped out of the parlor window, ran along a muddied trail for miles and almost made it to town but got detoured when I saw a dump truck overturned, blocking the auxiliary road. There I saw the driver of the dump truck crawling on the ground with shards of glass all over his body and blood gushing from his hands. The man must have seen me through the trees because he cried out, "Help! Me!"

I sprung up and charged down the other side of the marsh into unknown territory, hurdling over branches and unkempt debris with the duffle bag slung over my back. I didn't know where I was running to but being on the run made me feel alive. My brother Marshall would always say, 'self-conservation is the most notable instinct of man.' Within a half a mile I found an abandoned mill and stopped upon hearing a running creek that made a pleasant, soothing sound. After a minute though I heard a noise on the other side of the mill. It was a man preparing a fire. He noticed me and waved.

I tried to run away but instead tripped awkwardly on my right side, spraining my pelvis and cracking a rib. "Ahh motherfucker!" I roared, miserably, forcing myself up.

"Hey fella! You alright? I heard a racket." The man said, casually walking over. He wore camouflage clothing and had a brimmed straw hat to shield his face from the sun, which was now almost set. I had to get away from him. God forbid he recognized me.

"Yeah I'm alright, thanks!" I waved, tugging the bag across the dirt, but then lost my balance again and fell. The camouflage man ran to catch up with me and put his hand on my shoulder. He was so close, I was terrified.

"I have some 'Cetominifin over by my tent, give me a second."

I quenched my teeth before yelling, "I'm okay! Get away from me!" Then the camouflage man walked back across the mill towards his tent. I forced myself up now and dragged the bag against the dirt again, knowing that somewhere in my heart I had the strength to journey forward no matter what. But after a minute I lost my energy and sat down on a tree stump to ruminate:

I learned to have thick skin growing up in the Tri-Cities. Although the nature versus nurture argument never amused me, I still tended to be on the side of nurture, and my ego says how great I am for becoming a lawyer, although I still dreamed of a richer and fuller life, but not like those nitwit celebrities I'd watch in reality TV shows with my wife Malinda. She loved all those shows and said that those celebrities were like normal people because they lost their wealth to vices like booze, drugs and gambling. Then I wondered if it was really reality TV or self-mutilation. They even put cameras in the bathrooms sometimes. Now who'd want to see you taking a shit? And then they'd figure out some way to get rich again. I wouldn't mind the cameras I think. Even though I was on the other side of the law. Damn.. I had just realized my own limitations. My old philosophy professor would say something like, "You can't outrun the fabric of time and space." But I'd land myself in the grave before going to jail.

That's when Donald Eddy, The Creep, called me. I thumbed in my pocket, looking for my prepaid phone, not realizing I even had cell service here, but I recognized his number.

"What's up?" I answered hesitantly.

"Hey X, it's your best client."

"What do you want, Creep?"

Donald Eddy or better known as, The Creep, was a Brick City criminal, implicated fourteen times for employing underage workers and paying slave wages to them. He got out scot free though because he had the best lawyer each time (me). The Creep had my number on speed dial.

"I just got word that you're selling Mr. Frazier's diamonds. Lady Teacups said it's too good to be true, but I know you always deliver."

"This is a deal, Eddy. A million dollars for the lot. Sounds good?" I questioned.

"Yeah that's good. I have the money. But remember that if you screw me over on this deal, I'll have Mauricio, Alvarez, and Lady

Teacups skin you alive and barbecue you on the next St. Gennaro feast. Capeesh."

"Capeesh." I agreed, taking a pen from my pocket and writing down Eddy's (I mean The Creep's) number. "See you in three days Creep." I hung up and tossed the phone into the murky pool of water in the marsh. Better safe than sorry. Never know what the government is interfering with these days.

I attempted to walk once again, but got dizzy and almost fell. I kept my balance and looked down, noticing the duffle bag pulsating in my eye and changing colors. *Not another one of those sick visions.* I thought before hearing a faint voice coming from the bag. "This is yours. All the wealth you've ever desired. You won't keep us?"

"Fuck you!" I shouted.

"You ungrateful bitch!" The inanimate object screamed. In response I kicked the bag as hard as I could, aggravating my sprained ankle. "You motherfucker! You'll be The Creep's problem soon."

"Don't be so sure about that!" The bag responded.

IV

I noticed the camouflage man staring from a distance, he must have heard me shouting. I had a bad feeling. "Hey buddy! I got that Cetominifin." He said, running back over and holding out the medicine.

"I don't want your poison." I said, limping my way down the dirt trail, realizing I forgot where I was now. I turned back to face the camouflage man. "Actually sir can you help me with some directions to the nearest train station?"

"The nearest railroad is in Fulton." The man said, eyeing me up suspiciously. "It's funny though cause I've never seen a wanderer lost this deep in the bayou."

I contemplated a reply but couldn't think of anything. Thankfully, he brushed over that last remark and changed the subject.

"I'll make the trip to Fulton with you because the path is tricky to navigate." He said calmly. "It's not far though and when we get there I know a family pub where we can drink like kings on a budget. And I'm buying."

"No thanks."

"Hey mister.. I don't know what you've heard about Southern hospitality but I can't leave you in this shape. And it's getting dark soon, you probably don't even have a flashlight?"

"I don't."

"Well then you'd be dead in a minute, fall in a bog or get trapped by the Lochness. Let me grab a flashlight and put out my fire." The man came back in a few minutes, with a flashlight in his back pocket.

"So where you from up North?" The camouflage man asked, walking next to me.

"Born in Philly, grew up in Pittsburgh." I lied.

"You don't look like a Pittsburgh bloke. What's your name?"

"Roger…" I said, sweating. "What's yours?"

"Call me Lou," The camouflage man extended his hand. "It's a pleasure to make your acquaintance." He stared at me, silent, before asking, "You been up this way before Roger?"

"Well, I had an Aunt that used to live out here and I decided to venture down for nostalgia. But this place doesn't seem like how I remember it."

"Ain't really nothing noteworthy in the marsh… unless you like dead bodies." He said, creepily. "Can you believe we've had more bodies appearing around here lately? And the pub in Fulton will have all the news."

"As long as they serve food. I'm starved." I said, attempting to act calm. Honestly I would have enjoyed Lou's company, but he never stopped asking questions so I kept lying, unsure if he recognized my face and was scoping me out. So I spun such a web of lies that I began to fear I'd trip over my own stories soon enough. Then I felt the switchblade in my pocket, thinking the gambit was up and that was it, I should take care of him now.

"What are you lugging in that bag? Looks awfully heavy." My palm sweated on the knife as I was about ready to use it, then a large animal ran across our path and birds scattered in all directions. Luckily the beast didn't notice us. "See.. Good thing you got company Roger. It's unlikely the bigguns will bother us if we're together. And we're almost into town. The path ends right up ahead and leads to Main Street." I relaxed and loosened the grip of the blade in my pocket as we made it to Main Street. The pub was like he said only a few yards away.

"Here it is," he said. I read the sign which read, 'Mima's Tap. Southern famous beer and wings.'

We walked in. I noticed all the dining room tables empty and followed Lou as he walked past the dining room towards a long bar in the back. A man and a woman were behind the bar stocking liquor on the shelves. I kept my head down and stayed quiet.

"Hey there Mima and John. Where the kids?" Lou lifted his arm to wave and I got a good whiff of him now that we were in an enclosed space; he smelled worse than gas station cologne and onions.

"They're in the back cleaning the kitchen." the man replied. Lou nodded then looked up at the clock hung up on the side wall.

"I'm sorry, didn't realize the time, is you closed?" Lou asked.

"We're always open for you Lou. Thank you for your service." The woman said, before asking, "What can we get you for?"

"Two ice colds. Put 'em on my tab." Lou said, and sat on a bar stool. I, on the other hand, walked over to a dimly lit table in the corner of the pub and lounged back, almost tipping my chair over. Lou gave me that same look again from before and came over with the two beers in his hands. "Being awfully shy are you?" He said sitting in a chair next to me. I ignored him and sipped my beer.

After a couple minutes the man from the bar came over to the table with a notepad. Up close I saw he had red hair and freckled cheeks. He was young in his early thirties. "So how ya been Lou? Pretty late for you, coming from the trails? I heard a dump truck overturned by the landfill. Did you see anything?"

"Haven't heard. I was making a fire for the night when I ran into this fellow. Helping him navigate, before he hitches a train up North."

The woman, eavesdropping on our conversation, walked up to the table with a jug of water. "No late night ranting today Lou. Kids got school tomorrow." Lou chuckled and took a gulp of his beer. "I'm serious! I'll cut you off." She exclaimed heartily as two kids ran up to our table, a boy (nine) and a girl (seven).

"Mama, can we go upstairs now and watch the next episode of Animal Sanctuary. We did all our chores, except washing the table sheets, but we'll get up early tomorrow. Promise." The boy crossed his fingers behind his back, his little sister followed suit.

"No way! You kids don't realize how good you have it here. Tell 'em Lou, maybe they'll listen to you."

"But please Ma! This is the second to last episode." The little boy said.

As they were talking my face felt flush and one of those dizzy spells came on and I faded into a daydream of an open orchard and a large falcon flying towards me. I attempted to grab it, but instead it clawed my arm and I started bleeding. I grabbed the falcon with my other arm and tossed it on the ground and stomped on it.

While I was in this daydream the woman looked me up and down, recognizing me from the TV and the newspapers as the thief from the Tri-Cities.

"I thought I recognized you!" She shouted. Her convictions were firm, she ran behind the counter to call the police.

Then everything turned red and I saw my reflection in the mirror behind the bar; my face had blood and flesh all over it, and my clothes were stained like a butcher's cloak. Beside the mirror the woman's head lay, torn off at the neck, next to a full liter bottle of Johnny Walker. Lou sat face up at the table, dead, but still with blood gushing from his neck, and a hunting knife lay by his right side. Blood was all over the tables and the floors. But the duffle bag behind me was spotless.

'That bitch made you do it.' The bag said behind me. 'That bitch made you do it! That bitch made you do it!' Was all the bag kept saying.

"Shut up!" I turned and yelled. "It was you who made me do it, you fucking liar! It's been you this whole damned time!" I reached down and picked up the bloody knife, wielded it high in the air ready to cut into the pristine leather fabric of the bag.

"You better rethink that! If you ever want to see Selah and live happily ever after." The bag said. I was taken aback and dropped the knife as soon as I heard Selah's name.

"You're listening. Now follow everything I tell you. First, go over to the stove. And bring that bottle of Johnny Walker." I did as directed and fired on the stove. "Perfect, now drink. And when the stove is hot you'll know what to do." I drank the whole bottle in five minutes.

'None of them made a sound. None of them made a sound.' Those words rang in my ears as my head tilted to the right. I tried to balance but my whole body gave way putting me eye level with the countertop. 'There's a good girl, get me another drink Ms. Porkie.' I said, drunkenly staring at her severed head, like the spectacle it was, and taking the last swig of the Johnny Walker; then I tossed the bottle across the room; it smashed against the wall and knocked over an old dart board.

I stumbled up to the stove, gasping for air, and stood in front of it. All of a sudden knowing what I had to do. I placed my ten fingers right onto the stovetop, and scolded my fingerprints right off. I screamed in agony, and passed out from the immense pain.

V

I came to a few minutes later from the sound of police sirens approaching outside. The noise blaring into my sweaty, bloody, drunken head; the sound swung as if concluding a crescendo in a divine rhapsody. I couldn't face myself, realizing I was covered in blood; horrified my hands and clothes were soaked in their blood. I had no choice but to get up and hurry to the cash register at the end of the bar. I looked over my shoulder and saw the woman's head again, on the back mirror of the bar, her head next to my reflection. I opened the register, and took out a fistful of dollars and a few twenties. Enough so that I could run far... But before I could think of my next move, I didn't want to wind up like the rest of them... *How'd... I....?* They were all dead. And I couldn't stop looking at the two butter knives lodged into her husband's carotid artery. Instant, painless, blissful death. At least the family was all together.

I heard car doors slam outside, then muffled voices and the clobbering of footsteps. I froze, stuffing the money into my pockets and hid behind the bartop with the duffle bag by my side.

"County Police!" They banged on the front door of the pub. I looked out from behind the bar and saw Lou's flashlight sprawled on the floor. I jumped out to grab the flashlight just as three policemen barged into the establishment. They saw me immediately and fired bullets in my direction. I ducked back for cover behind the countertop with the flashlight in my hand.

"Come out, you're under arrest!" The three policemen said in unison, moving into the main room.

"Oh God!" Another cop said, seeing Mima's decapitated head next to the mirror.

"Holy shit!"

"Sick fuck!" The third cop said.

I quietly opened the small side pouch of my bag so I could tuck the flashlight inside but there was something else in that pocket. It was my brother Marshall's gun. "Never know when you're gonna need it." Marshall would have said.

I grabbed the gun and shot out from behind the bar counter, hitting one cop in the shoulder; he dropped his gun and held the wound with his hand.

"You have one more chance to come out!" The two other cops shouted, moving closer, missing me from point blank range and leaving bullet shells at my area beside the bar.

From my position I looked straight ahead out through a large window and saw a telephone pole with a street light and a large transformer can at the top.

"You'll never take me alive!" I said purposelessly.

"Listen pal! Before we kill you we're kicking the shit out of you! Then we're gonna stomp your face on the curb outside. You hear!"

I stared at the telephone pole again and looked into the gun chamber. I had *one shot left.* I prayed, aiming at the transformer can. BANG! The telephone pole ignited, causing the electricity on the whole street to blow out.

In the pitch black, I tossed my duffle bag through the window. It landed on the side lawn and I jumped out the window after it, picked it up and staggered down the street. The cops attempted a couple shots at me in the dark and one of the bullets grazed my head as I turned down a narrow alley, kicking aside trash cans and for a split second, checking out Fulton's best graffiti artists. I moved with purpose, just as my rib and leg pain began to muddle my vision. I had a pounding migraine too from hearing sirens roaring in every direction.

Across the street up ahead I saw a large crucifix adorning the front entrance to a graveyard. I disregarded the 'No Trespassing' sign and broke the padlock with the backside of my gun; the chain fell to the ground and I slid inside. Never been happier to be in a dark cemetery, couldn't help to think.

But the sirens were almost at the gates. I ran further just as the cops parked, stepped out of their vehicles and beamed their flashlights toward me. They entered the graveyard and ran up and down the rows of tombstones with their guns out. A couple bullets flew past my shoulder as I crouched behind a large statue. I scoured for an escape plan and noticed the cops attempting to surround me. The only credible idea I had was to run up to a crypt ten yards away. It was a small building with a brown door and an obelisk statue mounted above it. I ran to the door which said 'RIP FULTON FAMILY'. Then I jiggled the door handle. No luck. I slammed into it. It didn't budge.

Dammit!

I hurried to the side of the crypt to shield myself from more gunfire and even thought about jumping onto the roof, but then my eyes became fixed onto a metal gloss embroidery of letters that read: **Forever in our hearts.** I stared at the letters and my instinct told me to touch them even though I lost the sensation in my fingers. I pushed on the letters as hard as I could, and as soon as I did a small hole in the ground opened near my feet.

Meanwhile, the cops were getting closer and one of them shouted, "You sick fuck! We know you're back there! We got orders from the Tri-Cities to shoot to kill. There's a price tag on your head, dead or alive."

Hidden from sight, I shoved the duffle bag through the small hole in the ground, squeezing the sides so it could fit in. But in my attempt to get the bag inside the flashlight fell out of the side pocket onto the dirt. I didn't notice right away as I slid smoothly into the dark passageway. Then I thought about Lou's flashlight. I hugged the bag and reached into the pocket. Where's my flashlight? Dammit. I couldn't see anything. It had to be up on the dirt. I lifted my head up through the hole, still hidden from the policemen, and snagged the flashlight, hearing their muffled voices getting closer.

The strong beam from my flashlight illuminated the cavern. Immediately I noticed a small lever mounted on the rock to my left. I pulled it, and that closed the opening above. I was relieved but claustrophobic as the cavern was really tight and the path led down a steep and narrow stairway, so narrow that the pressure of the rocks etched into my body and the bag had an even harder time. How could anyone construct this place? Was my only coherent thought at the time.

I was a mess, bloody and achy, with two broken ribs, a sprained ankle, scolded fingerprints and a headache that wouldn't forgive. I kept the flashlight shining directly in front of me so I wouldn't miss a step and fall to my death. I moved slowly, dragging the heavy bag, using as much muscle as I could to reach the bottom of the steps which led to a wider room.

The loud noises from outside faded away now. But the walls began to vibrate and small pebbles fell off the chiseled rock onto the ground, creating a cloud of dust. When I reached the bottom of the steps, I saw a table with a red tablecloth, and five skeletons (looked like three women and two young children) sitting together at the table and died holding hands. I held my mouth with my blood soaked hand, then put my other hand on my forehead and tried to hold back from vomiting. The room smelled of decay, it was bad but not as bad as Lou smelt earlier.

Then the room became foggy and an apparition appeared. It was that same pale figure that I had seen at Uncle Charlie's place. "Told you to count on me." It said.

"What!?" I jumped, not sure if I was more startled at seeing the ghost or the skeletons. And by now I couldn't even think because the stench of the room was so overpowering.

"There's a map inside the main pouch of your bag. It will lead you back to the Tri-Cities." The pale figure spoke thunderously.

"But.." I tried to speak.

"Don't ask questions. This is dire. And I have orders to assist you."

"But there's no map here, I'm sure…." My fingers struggled to open the main compartment of the bag. But when I did, there it was on top of all the diamonds, a small map with a red marker outlining an underground trail.

That map definitely wasn't there before, I was sure of that.

"There's a tunnel down here from an abandoned pipeline that leads to Brick City. It's all on the map. You better go now because Selah is in danger."

Then the pale, mysterious figure disappeared.

Part II

I

The spirit of Sir Sophus Penn appeared in a banquet hall, sitting at the head of an endless table, where thousands of other spirits were present.

"Divine Counsel, pardon me for calling this meeting. As you know, it is I, Sir Penn, here to request protection for Xavier."

A flame ignited in the center of the table and spoke, "Well Sophus, there is no need for you to speak as we have already read all your thoughts. As for Xavier, he has chosen his fate."

Sir Penn shouted at the flame: "No! He deserves better!"

"On behalf of this council," the flame continued, "I must say we appreciate your bravery, humbleness and confidence to supplicate such a request. We know you have a generous heart, and that is why you are here at this table; however, Xavier is on his own, there is nothing we can do for him." The flame grew larger and engulfed the entire table, the voice that spoke from it was now thunderous. "I'm afraid this is a bigger mission than you realize."

II

Sir Penn's clothes were torn, his mind rattled, and spirit shaken not stirred. He recalled an impression of a dream in his mind as he stared down Lexington Avenue in Brick City, craving food and water. Then a drunken man ran up to him waving a newspaper, and shouted, "Get off of my corner you illiterate!"

"Where am I?" Sir Penn said.

"Brick City. And for being on my corner," the drunken man slurred, "you must pay me a pint of bourbon for good measure."

Sir Penn fumbled in his empty pockets, scouring up some lint. "I've got nothing. Sorry." He showed the man the insides of his pockets.

"If you got nuffin' you better get out. This is my corner chump." The man raised his newspaper to swat Sir Penn away, "Pitiful. Pitiful." He said, contorting his face, desperately in need of a pint of bourbon.

"Please. I need to get home." Sir Penn held his arm up to push the man away.

The drunken man held his balance, remembering he had a flask in his back pocket. He snatched it up, put it to his lips, and searched for a last drop. But he had already exhausted his supply. "You mean the homeless shelter? Keep going down Lexington until you reach Main, turn right and you'll see a barricade. That's how they keep the police away. All you need to do is crawl underneath."

"Is that where you live?" Sir Penn asked him.

"No, I live here on this corner!"

"But how do I get to the Tri-Cities?"

"Good luck!" The drunken man said, teetering and muttering down the sidewalk.

Sir Penn continued walking down Lexington Ave, where the sidewalk was covered in food scraps, soda cans and cigarette butts. He happened to pick up a newspaper among a pile of debris on the ground and read the headline: **'Marshall killed by his brother Xavier in San Antonio. Diamonds missing!'** And underneath was a picture of Xavier, the famous lawyer from Alistor Street. Sir Penn lost his balance and slammed into the front window of a shoe store. He was losing his energy and used all his strength to brace himself against a window where men's dress shoes and womens high heel shoes were displayed.

Meanwhile a woman parked her car on the street and recognized his face. She got out and screamed. "Penn!" He looked over but was blinded by the light of the sunrise reflecting off her beige sedan. "What the hell are you doing out here?" She continued. "Everyone thought you were dead. Didn't you drown?" Sir Penn attempted to speak. "Are you a junkie now?" She questioned. "Ahha! That's why you disappeared, so you could go back to the *grisly*? Damn it Penn, get a grip on yourself!"

"No. No." He said, expelling all his energy to hold himself up.

"You of all people! You're the last person I thought would take part in the *grisly*, you know how many people die every year of overdoses."

"Sh…shut…. up," he mumbled. "No... ne… need…. food…" he tried to say. "and…. water…." Then he lost his balance.

"I shouldn't be doing this, but…" She felt compassionate for him. "Come inside my office. I'll grab you food from upstairs. You'll just have to wait in the lobby for a minute." Selah worked in Accounts Payable for Lucky's Packing Company on Lexington Ave in Brick City. She was their most honorable employee, young, smart, sexy and always in good spirits. Today she wore a floral red dress, high heel shoes and a gold cross necklace. Her hair was done up with a pin through it and her bony cheekbones exemplified her flush face. She went back to her car and grabbed a heavy box filled with papers.

"Follow me, the building is this way." She held the front door of her building open with her back as Sir Penn limped over balancing against the storefront windows.

"Come on Penn this is heavy. If anything you should be carrying this for me." Sir Penn caught up, but collapsed as soon as he got into the threshold of the building.

"Good morning Parsons," Selah greeted the security guard sitting at his desk immersed in a binge worthy Netflix show.

"Hiya Selah!" He perked up and paused the episode. "Happy Monday. How was your three day weekend?"

"It was an eventful one. Did you see the news?" Selah asked.

"Oh yeah, it seems like everyone's gone mad," Parsons said, staring up at Selah, not yet noticing Sir Penn facedown on the floor. "Can you believe my annoying neighbors came to my backyard party for the second year in a row. I told my wife not to invite them yet she did anyway I think just to spite me." Parsons shook his head as Selah passed through the metal detector with her cardboard box. The buzzer rang hysterically. "Don't worry hun, go ahead." Selah smiled, continued through the vestibule and made her way into the main lobby. Now Parsons noticed Sir Penn lying on the floor comatose. "Hey hold on Selah!" He yelled. "Did you notice this junkie on the floor behind you? Or am I seeing things again? These long nights get the best of me."

"Yeah, I'm sorry Parsons. He's an old friend. I'm gonna get him something from upstairs then he'll be on his way. I promise." The lines on the forehead of Parsons's disgruntled face furrowed.

"Well, you know I'd do anything for you Selah, but this is a bad look for the building."

"Please just a minute."

"Okay. Make it quick." He nodded.

"No one is here this early anyway Parsons, you know I'm always two hours early."

"I know you are. 7:30 sharp, every morning. And you don't clock in until 9:30? You must be a saint if I ever knew one." He winked at her. "Now hurry up cause this has been a long minute."

Selah headed over to the elevator and elbowed the button, causing the cardboard box to almost slip out of her grip; but she re-gripped it in time and waited patiently at the door.

When the elevator door opened, an inconspicuous gentleman walked out, wearing a wide brimmed hat. He kept his head down concealing his face. He carried a large briefcase and she noticed a lightning bolt tattoo on his neck as he passed by. She glanced at the security desk but Parsons wasn't sitting there anymore.

"Wonder who that was." She thought, shrugging it off and getting on the elevator, pressing the 7th floor button, and praying she'd make it in one piece as the elevator always rattled its entire way up. *They better fix this thing before there's an issue*, she thought. After she stepped out onto the 7th floor she looked at her watch, *it's been three minutes, hopefully Parsons isn't complaining.* She turned on the lights and immediately noticed the main office door ajar. She peered in and saw papers scattered all over the floor. Mr. Locklard's office had been tampered with, and all his filing cabinets ransacked. Her heart beat faster than ever as a vision of the man with the lightning bolt tattoo flashed in her mind. She dropped the box of papers and phoned Parson's from her desk. She waited, but the phone line was busy. Meanwhile, she made sure her desk was untouched. Everything looked in order, she didn't have much besides an inspirational quote calendar, an organizer for pens and a picture of all twenty seven of her nieces and nephews (she had nine siblings). She kept her work area plain and simple and free from clutter. Then she re-dialed Parsons for a second time.

Parsons answered now, "Hey Selah I knew you were coming right back. But I stepped away for a second and I don't see your friend now."

"What! Where'd he go?!" She interjected.

"I'm not sure. I just went to the surveillance room because one of the camera feeds went down. I checked to see if the cables were plugged in correctly and when I came back your friend wasn't here anymore."

Selah froze in shock. "You said some of the camera feeds went down? But did you happen to see someone walking out with a large briefcase?"

"I didn't see anyone. Why what's wrong?"

"Well Locklard's office on the 7th floor has been ransacked, his desk and filing cabinets were broken into and I saw a man walk out of the elevator on the first floor before I got on."

"Oh shit! You better get down here to be safe, I'm calling the cops."

. . .

The man with the lightning bolt tattoo walked into the vestibule just as Parsons stepped away.

Sir Penn saw him approaching. *Why's that man walking so fast with that briefcase?*

When the man got closer he gave Sir Penn a steel toe boot straight into his face. POP.

III

Sir Penn was jolted in the backseat of an all black 2013 Cadillac CTS with decked out rims, tinted windows and red leather interior. His arms and legs were tied. He could tell by the pressure of the rope that it was a fisherman's knot. "How are you feeling back there?" A recognizable voice came from the driver's seat.

"Where are you taking me?" Sir Penn replied, his hunger faded temporarily. The demands of his body could wait.

"The big guy on Alistor Street wants to see you." The driver pulled a quick left turn.

"Why don't you go down Ironbound?" The man in the passenger seat asked.

"Trust me, that way is loaded with cops in plain clothes. They'll spot this car by the drop of a dime. They might already be on the lookout." The driver wiped his forehead and turned to the man with the lightning bolt tattoo on his neck. "You said you saw the girl too?" He asked.

"Yeah, but it was just for a second. And she saved us time dragging this clown in the building."

"Yeah but she probably called the cops already. We can't afford interference... Or the boss will have both our heads stuffed."

Sir Penn woke up suddenly and yelled over the top of them, "What the hell do you think you're doing!"

"Shut your mouth until we get to Alistor Street. The boss will set you straight. He told us you were hiding out in Brick City."

"Whoever had on the steel toe boots had better kill me because I don't forget a grudge." Sir Penn said.

The man in the passenger seat turned around, his eyebrows looked stenciled, and glared at Sir Penn. "Yeah, is that right?" Then he punched Penn right in the mouth, causing blood to gush from his lip.

"Thanks Sparky. Thought he'd never shut up!" The man in the driver's seat said.

Sparky was a military retiree and a Tri-Cities electrician. He earned a reputation over the years as a copper thief, stealing from every project he worked on until reprimanded, after getting caught cutting down copper from telephone poles in the middle of the night on storm duty. That was before Sparky got a job working for the 'Big Guy' on Alistor Street.

The Cadillac continued down a discreet neighborhood of Brick City, and passed two undercover cop cars. Luckily, the cops inside both cars had their heads down and slept with sunglasses on. "You were right Alin! Good job with the detour. We might have been cornered the other way."

"And we're safe going through Walden?" Sparky asked.

"Yeah cause it's on the Southside." Alin replied, referring to a small inconspicuous road, hidden behind a pickleball court, and used only for gang and drug related activities between Brick City and the Tri-Cities. The road was near the Walden school district and heavily guarded by an anarchist militia called The Force, who were paid off in advance by the Big Guy. Good thing he was loaded.

"All you need is a little money to solve the most strenuous of problems," Alin said.

"Touche." Sparky agreed as they drove on a maintenance road around the back of the Walden middle school where the pickleball courts were on the left. They approached a tall and wide concrete wall at the end of the road. And miraculously, a narrow passage in the wall began opening, just large enough to squeeze a small car in. "If we bring this back with a scratch you know he'll never forget about it." Alin drove slowly and the side mirrors almost scraped.

The passage led them onto Egenof Ave, in the Eastside section of Elizabeth, the oldest of the three cities that made up the Tri-Cities (Elizabeth, Roselle and Linden), where public service workers were still cleaning up the streets of garbage, remnants of the massive July 4th celebration weekend.

"What a fucking weekend this was, huh?" Sparky remarked.

Alin shrugged his shoulders, swerving left and right to dodge debris from garbage trucks so overloaded that all the garbage that had just been picked up was again flying all over the place.

Alin crossed Broad Street as the clock on the dashboard said 8AM. The train from the Elizabeth station screeched in the background and pedestrians ran from all directions hoping to catch it and head to work.

After half a mile, Alin turned left onto Alistor Street, which was located in the Elegant North section of the Tri-Cities, where every year the houses became larger and larger through construction renovations. Most of the houses now had wraparound patios, landscape lighting, and inground swimming pools. They passed by Xavier's old home, now a pile of rubbish and ash blocked off with caution tape. "What a shame Malinda got herself into marrying that crook Xavier." Sparky said.

From there they saw Old Leman already out on the corner betting on a dice game, taking off his watch and placing it as his next bet, as an elderly woman walked past with her three-legged beagle on a leash. Leman stopped to hit on her but she yelled for him to stay away.

Alin, driving by, rolled down his window to shout, "Hey Leman!"

"Yo Alin! Tell Mr. Frazier when I see him I'm gonna kick his ass!" Leman stuck out both middle fingers. Alin then made it up to a rustic fence with large silver-plated letters that read FRAZIER. The gates were motion sensored for Mr. Frazier's twenty-two vehicles. Frazier's carport was the size of a gymnasium located underneath the Frazier mansion. The Cadillac that Alin drove was the least expensive of Frazier's collection ranging from Porsches, Bentleys, Ferraris, and Bugattis. Alin sped down the driveway up to a front courtyard with a huge thirteen foot tall angel statue standing in the center, its wings spanning five feet wide on each side of its body. The angel was surrounded by flowers of all shapes, colors and sizes. Alin drove around it and up to the front door where Stephen, a young tall red haired Irishman, stood expecting them.

"Why Mr. Frazier has been awfully impatient, what's taken so long." Stephen said as Sparky jumped out of the car, opened the backdoor, pulled out Sir Penn and tossed him onto the pavement. Then Sparky grabbed the briefcase from the trunk and placed it down.

The large cathedral doors of the mansion opened and Mr. Frazier walked out. He saw Sir Penn on the ground, grabbed him by the shirt collar and pulled him like a dog towards the door. "Hey Stephen," Mr. Frazier called over to his butler. "Grab that briefcase and put it in the back office near my desk." Stephen obeyed orders and carried the briefcase inside.

"Sparks what the hell were you thinking? I told you to be out of that building by 7:30! The woman saw you on the elevator. They'll have a sketch of you on the evening news." Mr. Frazier pulled out a pistol from his back pocket. Then from his other pocket he took out a silencer attachment and screwed it onto the barrel of the pistol, and pointed the gun at Sparky.

"I'm sorry boss, I made a mistake, I'll skip town." Sparky said.

IV

Mr. Frazier pulled the trigger and shot Sparky in the chest twice. Sparky dropped like the New Year's Eve ball at Times Square.

"Alin good work. You're definitely getting that bonus I promised you, mark my words." Frazier said, unscrewing the silencer and sticking the gun and the attachment into his pocket. "Now take care of this body."

"I got it boss, don't worry. I'll bag him up and dump him into the Warachando lake."

"Perfect!" Frazier said, before pulling Sir Penn by the collar again and proceeding into the house.

"I'm actually happy to see you." Mr. Frazier said, tossing Sir Penn onto the couch of his back parlor. Then Frazier opened the briefcase that his butler laid out. He took out all the papers and threw them onto his desk. The papers in the briefcase contained Lucky's Packing Company's domestic and international personal bank account numbers. Frazier couldn't wait to wipe out their accounts and watch Mr. Locklard's company crash and burn. "At least Sparky was good for some things." He said, pulling out a cigarette from his beige sport coat. "Sir, you missed the fun we had the last few days! What happened to you?"

Sir Penn's eyes were bloodshot from exhaustion as he glanced over at the large man, Mr. Leopold Frazier, the European emigrant who rose to be the richest man in the Tri-Cities. Frazier was always in a decent mood as long as he had what he wanted.

"So… Penn. Are you going to cooperate? Or do I have to take care of you like I did Sparky?" Mr. Frazier's hands seemed to swallow the entire cigarette.

"Please," Sir Penn mumbled, "need food and drink."

"Ahhhhh… so that's all it takes to get the magnificent Sir Penn to speak his mind." Frazier took a few long puffs. "Stephen!" Frazier yelled out.

"Yes sir." Stephen reported promptly in the doorway.

"Go fetch our guest here some food to freshen his spirit. Anything will do…" Frazier shooed him off.

"I'll be right back." Stephen ran.

Meanwhile, Sir Penn felt like the incarnation of death, tied up uncomfortably in a sitting position, his eyes drooped and his head tilted at a forty five degree angle, with dried blood on his face, shirt and pants. If he hadn't weathered ten years in a couple of hours, he would pass for a handsome gentleman. "What happened to Xavier's house?" Sir Penn questioned.

"That's two more questions than you should be asking. First tell me how you wound up on Lexington Ave." Frazier puffed a huge cloud of smoke right in Sir Penn's face, but the smoke didn't affect him.

Now Stephen walked in carrying a serving tray with a tea kettle, a china cup and a bran muffin on it. And placed the tray on a beautiful coffee table, handcrafted of oak wood and sapphire embroidery right in front of Sir Penn who was hungrier than a lumberjack on a new vegan diet. "Watch that table!" Frazier shouted. "It cost me $45,000 at the auction over the weekend!"

Sir Penn squirmed in his tied up position. He was able to get his face near the tray and felt like a dog about to bite into the muffin.

"Please untie him! I'd love to watch him struggle but he'll leave a mess everywhere."

Once Stephen untied him, Sir Penn lunged towards the plate and swallowed the muffin whole.

"I don't know Leo." Penn answered after almost choking. "Honestly it felt like I had died and woke up from The Big Sleep. I didn't know where I was." Sir Penn said before reaching for his tea.

"Only addicts who spike the *grisly* into their veins land on Lexington Ave. And it's not too far-fetched since you've been there before..."

"I ain't no addict if that's what you're implying. I answered you truthfully Leo, now you answer my question."

Mr. Frazier laughed, turning away, "Not a chance. I don't listen to street rats." Then he peered out the bay windows into his backyard orchard, took off his sport coat, the cufflinks on his dress shirt shining from the light coming through the windows. The morning heat warmed up the room. "Today I shall speak in front of the Tri-City council.' Frazier said. "The *New*, New Reform Bill will be voted into effect."

"Are you an idiot? Don't you learn from your mistakes Leo?" Sir Penn interjected.

"Mark my words Sir Sophus Penn! I will get my revenge. I know Xavier's still alive and I have a tip that he's heading back to Brick City to sell those diamonds." Mr. Frazier looked out at the massive Wall Street bull in the middle of the orchard, his most expensive purchase to date at ten million dollars, which he bought in order to help bail out a few financial companies in the New York Stock Exchange collapse last year. "You know I always admired Xavier and how he became a lawyer, but crossing me was the stupidest thing he ever did. Once you find him, bring him to me."

"I'd never! We've been friends for twenty years."

"Well that's the fun part. It's either bring him here within forty eight hours or you're dead."

Sir Penn, flabbergasted, poured another cup of tea and looked around the room, becoming more alert as nutrients entered his bloodstream. He scanned the massive library covering two walls, reading each title quickly like a computer processor: philosophy books, classic novels, poetry collections, erotic magazines, and handbound journals. Now he perceived an array of stuffed animal heads mounted high up on the walls, each had a small plaque underneath that said 'Courtesy of Anthony's Taxidermy'. And a stuffed caribou head, largest of them all, mounted directly above where Frazier stood.

"I'll let you take the Cadillac. The plates are unregistered." Frazier mumbled under his breath.

"Fuck you and your Cadillac." Sir Penn responded impudently.

Mr. Frazier looked up in shock. "Well just so you know my men stuck a tracker up your ass! So you're welcome to go any way you please. But you still have 48 hours. If Xavier isn't here by then, being dead will be a blessing for you."

Penn's left eyebrow twitched. "Fuck you!"

"I'll tell Stephen to give you a few bucks to catch the bus. And also an untapped phone so we can stay in touch." Frazier said, walking away. "See you in two days. Make me proud."

Sir Penn closed his eyes on the sofa, hoping for the real Big Sleep. Again.

V

Sir Penn was in a dream, staring down an eerie hallway. He noticed an array of doors on each side of the hall. But one of the doors was peculiar flashing a bioluminescent light. He stood still, watching the light fade in and out, then all of a sudden the light stopped, which intrigued him even more.

He sprinted along the hallway (which smelled like rat piss), and made it to the front of the door, now fully illumined, glowing brighter and brighter. There was a sign on the door that said **LOYALTY** in bold letters. He reached for the door knob, opened it and stepped inside.

Now he was in the middle of a heavy rainstorm without a jacket, recognizing that he was in the Tri-Cities on Broad Street at the commuter hour, because people were pacing up and down with their suitcases, raincoats and umbrellas. In the midst of the chaos he saw a young homeless boy wearing a tank top, gym shorts and torn sandals sitting on the curb crying, getting drenched by rain. The boy looked to be six or seven, and nobody cared that he was hurt.

Sir Penn ran over and realized immediately that the kid had a broken leg and couldn't walk. So he lifted the boy up on his right shoulder and sprinted toward St. Elizabeth's hospital, weaving in and out of pedestrians on the street, when he was almost blindsided by an elderly man who popped out of nowhere. "Hey watch it pal." The fellow mouthed at him. Sir Penn paid him no attention and kept zig-zagging between people on the sidewalk. From a quarter mile away, a bright red sign said 'EMERGENCY ROOM ENTRANCE', and large yellow letters 'CAUTION 15 MPH' stenciled into the pavement leading to the hospital. To his right, was a long processional gate and a toll booth where a guard sat with his legs up on the desk, trying to keep his eyes open.

Then sirens pierced his eardrums as an ambulance drove onto the hospital campus; the guard opened the gate and the ambulance stopped in front of the Emergency Room doors. There Sir Penn watched two EMTs come out wheeling a young boy on a stretcher into the hospital.

Wait, that looks like the kid I'm holding. Penn looked to his shoulder and realized the boy was no longer there. He glanced at the stretcher again, this time he recognized the young boy as a younger version of himself.

"Save him, hurry up!" He yelled at the EMTs. They ignored him and continued rolling the cart into the hospital. Sir Penn followed, unseen by security, he made it all the way into the operating room and stood next to a surgeon about to perform an emergency operation.

At that moment another surgeon calmly walked into the room, wearing a name tag that said *Travailleur de lumière*. Everyone else had ignored him, but this new surgeon stared directly into Sir Penn's eyes, penetrating him to the soul, saying, "You thought we'd let you die out there but our loyalty is deep, the only prerequisite is that you believe." The new surgeon moved closer to show his benevolent face, illuminated like energy from the sun, and continued, "I've been sent by your angels to fashion this message into your subconscious mind."

"What message?" Sir Penn asked.

"Believe and live by the truth of your heart. And never fret because your angels will help you in all types of trouble." Sir Penn stared at the new surgeon, who now began to fade away from view, vanishing like an apparition.

. . .

Sir Penn woke up drooling on the couch in the Frazier mansion. Stephen, the butler, stood over him holding an envelope that contained a few $20 bills and an untapped, burner phone. "Here. Better get on moving. You only have forty two hours left." Stephen handed Sir Penn the envelope and pointed him towards the doorway.

VI

Mr. Locklard fumed as all of his business information was stolen. He was in financial ruin, sitting in the interrogation room next to Selah.

"One in a million chance they find him." Mr. Locklard looked defeated. He was a man in his late 40's, normally optimistic, with a prominent jaw and large cheekbones. Today his eyes were dark foreboding circles. He threw his water cup at the wall in frustration. "Everything I've worked so hard for... Gone. In an instant!"

"Thankfully I got a good look at him. He was awfully scrawny and that neck tattoo stood out." Selah hoped she gave the cops the best description she could, as the images from this morning kept flashing in her mind. "Do you really think a couple of papers will determine the end of your business?"

"Selah." Mr. Locklard said in a monotone voice. "My accounts have been wiped out. That money took me decades to acquire." His head collapsed into his arms, he couldn't hold back the tears. "The world is awfully bleak."

One of the sergeants of the precinct burst into the room; a large, towering man of olive complexion, 6' 4", 250 pounds, wearing a tight police uniform. He opened his mouth and stared below at his detainees, his tongue touched the right side of his lip. "So before we cut you loose." He looked up at the fluorescent light hanging from the ceiling tile then back at Selah and Mr. Locklard sitting at the table. "Is there anyone else that could be a potential suspect?" He asked.

Mr. Locklard shook his head. "Only Mr. Frazier has the balls to pull off something like this."

The Sergeant began to choke. "You better hold your breath right there Mr. Locklard. If word gets out that Frazier was behind this there'll be more riots. Mark my words."

"Couldn't you just ask him some questions?" Selah asked innocently.

"Not without probable cause, or it'll be my last day working in the Brick City precinct. I'd end up in the Hudson River for even suggesting the idea."

"But you agree it's possible?" Locklard asked.

"You're out of your mind. Why would the wealthiest man in the Tri-Cities risk his career and livelihood to steal a few million from a small packing company?"

"Well…." Mr. Locklard looked over at Selah. "I believe this is payback for Container 66. That was our shipment that stored the diamonds… before they were stolen." As he said this the door opened again and a lanky gentleman in a police uniform poked his head in, his nose was so large he looked like he could sniff out a drug factory a mile away.

"Sergeant. I just got a call from the Tri-Cities. They found a body at the Warachando Lake matching the young lady's description. Tri-City police say they'll handle the rest. They want us to escort Mr. Lockard and Ms. Rosado to the border."

"Thank God. Looks like we'll be washing our hands of this case." The sergeant wiped the accumulation of sweat off his brow, then folded up his notebook, and stuffed it into his vest pocket. "Be outside in five minutes, the both of you." The Sergeant and the other officer walked out, leaving the door ajar.

"See Mr. Locklard. I told you this will all work itself out. Keep up your Faith." Selah said, patting him on the back, giving him the tenderness that he needed. Mr. Locklard never married anyone except his work and inwardly accepted that he'd die alone.

"Thanks Selah. It's reassuring that you're here." He forced his head up from his arms, his face crimson.

"It's the least I could do, boss. For you took me under your wing when I really needed a job. Honestly, how could I ever repay you?"

He stared into her eyes. "Oh Selah. I love you so much." He struggled not to cry. "I've loved you since the first day I met you."

Now her face turned crimson as well. "Well isn't this the time. What are you trying to say boss?"

"I'm crazy about you Selah. You're the only one I have ever truly loved and it hurts me more and more everyday that we are not together."

"You're delirious, get yourself together Mr. Locklard. Business is your true love! I've seen the way your eyes sparkle when you make a new deal."

"But no you don't understand. I am in love with you." He pleaded.

"I love you dearly, believe me. But not in the way you're expressing. I'm sorry." She desperately wanted to change the subject. Thankfully, the lanky officer stood before them near the door frame, with his arms straight down his side, almost touching his kneecaps.

"What's the hold up? We're waiting." He said.

VII

They walked down the main hall of the precinct where cops sat behind their desks, taking their morning nap, even though phones were ringing non-stop.

"I got a house of pigs and a city where addicts are dying by the truckload. All my officers are tired from the overtime that we're too greedy to deny. Officer Alvarez and I have worked seventy two hours straight!" The Sergeant yawned. "Our morgues are packed, cemeteries overfilled and cremation services are on a waiting list.

"Death breeds cash," The lanky officer said.

"What a shame," Selah chimed in. "So sad."

"Yeah it really is. We had to barricade off the whole Rahway district as the addicts over there were acting like zombies. Now we call them 'fallen angels of the fourth kind.' Make sure you're careful princess." The sergeant said, staring at the petite Selah, who stood gracefully in the center of the precinct with her red dress and high heels.

But Selah became irate: "I know I wear a skimpy dress and cute high heels, but don't be fooled.. Cause I'll drop kick anybody. You boys don't know anything about me." she stared at Mr. Locklard, then back at the sergeant. "And that goes for all your officers. I'll knock their shiny badges right off their dry cleaned uniforms." She caused a few officers in the precinct to awaken from their naps.

"Where'd you pick up this woman? Give her a badge, Sarge. She'd do well on the force." The detective, Dick Sordenburg, peered beyond the cubicle wall of his desk, sipping his coffee.

"Shut up Dick, and instead of remarks, maybe you can answer a damn phone before the Captain wakes up for his 2:30 meeting with the Fire Chief."

"I got a stack of court cases to review that line up from here to Kawaku. Maybe this afternoon I'll get on the phone. What's for lunch by the way? Let's pick up from that burger joint again."

"We'll discuss that when I get back. First we have to drop these two off at the Border Crossing."

The Sergeant, the lanky officer, Mr. Locklard and Selah Rosado proceeded to the main door and exited the building. They all sat inside a patrol car parked out front. The sergeant fired up the ignition and sped off down Lexington Avenue passing the building where Lucky's Packing Company was located. They continued onto Main Ave until they made it to the border crossing, and stopped at the gate as twenty two Tri-City police officers stood staring at the Brick City cop car.

A dark-skinned officer, with a fat lip of tobacco under his tongue, wearing circular sunglasses walked up to their car. "No entry for Brick City personnel." He said, then spit right onto the hood of their police vehicle.

The Sergeant, unphased, responded, "This is Mr. Edwin Locklard, CEO of Lucky's Packing Company, and his secretary Selah Rosado. We are officially handing this case over to your city."

The dark-skinned Tri-City officer pulled up his shades, showing his light blue eyes. "Alright leave 'em here. And you Brick City goons get out! Just looking at you makes me sick."

"Good luck." The Sergeant said to Mr. Locklard and Selah as they exited the vehicle. Once they got out, the sergeant wasted no time and sped off back to the Brick City precinct, screeching his tires, and leaving behind a cloud of smoke and the smell of burnt rubber.

Meanwhile, a group of Tri-City cops grabbed Mr. Locklard and escorted him into a small building beside the border gate. "Where are you taking him!" Selah shouted, amidst the chaos of the large plume of smoke rising.

The officers left her standing there for a few minutes, and gawked at her beautiful figure as she stood elegantly, fluttering her dress, until she finally grew impatient enough to stomp her heels repeatedly into the asphalt.

"Okay miss, show us your documents." One of the Tri-City officers called her over to a security booth window.

"I have my license, but my car is parked at my office on Lexington Ave in Brick City."

"Your car is official police evidence and is in our possession. And if everything checks out you will have it back in the next seven days. For now though, Lieutenant Conners will escort you to your home in Roselle." The officer winked and pointed to his left at a Tri-City police vehicle. "That's Conners sitting in there, he'll take care of you." She walked over to the car, recognizing the officer from the night of the fire, then she wondered if Mr. Locklard was okay. She was sick to her stomach in doubt, and stayed silent the entire ride, even though Conners tried to make small talk. Conners made a left onto Greene Street and then a right onto Alistor Street.

There it is. Selah rubbernecked as they passed by the horrifying remnants of the house fire from the other night. She couldn't help but wonder instinctively about Xavier and if he was okay on the run from the law. Now Conners continued up to Broad Street, passing Warachando Park where large ornately cut hedges spelt out the words **Welcome to Roselle.**

Conners parked right in front of Selah's house: 555 5th Ave.

"Be careful Ms. Rosado, that's twice in one week you've been in police custody." Officer Conners said before driving away.

VIII

She shrugged off the comment since she had done nothing wrong and walked up to her front porch. She fumbled for the keys in her purse and was startled to see Sir Penn hidden in the corner of the porch crouched behind a large Bamboo Paradise Palm Tree.

"What the hell Penn?"

"Shhh. Be quiet. Let's talk inside." He whispered as his legs quivered from kneeling in an awkward position for a prolonged period.

She composed herself and searched for her keys, which were all the way on the bottom of her purse; she fingered around until she pulled out a key ring loaded with souvenir key chains. She opened the door, whispering. "Quick. Run in."

He barrel rolled inside, landing on his face just behind the living room couch. "Shut the door." He said in a high-spirited tone.

"You better start talking!" Her tone became tense once the door was shut. "Explain to me how you got here from Brick City? There is no way they let you cross the border."

"Don't repeat a word of this.. But I just left Mr. Frazier's. And I know it was his plan to rob those files this morning."

"I knew it! Now we've got him, I'll call the police."

"No. No." Sir Penn jumped up and waved his hands maniacally. "We can't call the police."

"Why can't we?" She asked.

"Because Mr. Frazier is on the hunt for the diamonds. You know he will kill anyone that gets in his way."

"Shut up!" Her mouth flung open. She glared at Sir Penn as he sat on the couch and sprawled out his legs.

"Yeah. And I figured you of all people would know where to find Xavier." She had a blank expression and shook her head. He tried to read her thoughts. But no luck.

"I don't, and I have no intention of getting involved with him again." She remarked. "But I still don't understand why Mr. Frazier is also going after Mr. Locklard?"

Sir Penn stood up to stretch his back and replied, "I think Frazier needs to make sure everyone knows he's still the top dog in the Tri-Cities."

"I'm scared Penn. Not just for Xavier, or Mr. Locklard, but especially for the city." As she said this her cell phone rang. "Excuse me, let me see who this is." She walked over to the kitchen with her phone and spoke softly so Sir Penn couldn't hear. After a minute she re-entered the living room and said, "You wouldn't believe it… Xavier just called."

"What?"

"Yeah he's in Brick City," She said worriedly.

"Did he say where in Brick City?"

"Somewhere near the Plaza Hotel. And he said that I'm in danger and I should meet him right away."

"You're not thinking about it are you? He's a felon, you guys wouldn't get very far if you ran together." Sir Penn said.

"Of course not!" She shook her head. "I couldn't," she supplicated. "I'd never trust him again after everything."

"I think that's wise."

"But I still love him," He watched as tears welled up in her eyes.

"Stay inside and lock all the doors. I gotta go Selah. There's someone I need to meet up with before it gets too late. I'll give you a call in the morning."

Part III

I

Richard Prospere looked up from his bed made of feathers inside the Elizabeth freight train depot. He heard the last cargo load for the day down the tracks, making its way into Brick City. The sunset in his view left a last glimmer of purplish red light, fading into the encompassing dark. He grew accustomed to this, and began to enjoy his nightly routine as he reached over to grab his satchel. He felt the rugged burlap, rummaged through debris inside until he found a half banana and an overripe apple. He was low on food, also part of his nightly routine.

Somehow Rich stayed in good spirits, even though his wife kicked him out for shacking up with Caitlin Fernwood, the street floozy. Rich came home that day four months ago to find all his belongings on the front lawn, and all the door locks changed, which left him no choice but to load up his Subaru hatchback and ride off into the unknown. He finally felt free and started his journey blasting 'Free Bird' on the Garden State Parkway. He took a construction detour off the highway and onto River Drive until he was a mile or so from the Brick City border. But then his car engine backfired, leaving him stranded on the side of the road. He turned the key to start the motor again but all he heard was a loud grinding sound. He stepped out into the middle of the empty road and waved his arms helplessly seeing headlights coming towards him. And within seconds he heard the screeching axles of a tractor trailer approaching. But the driver was distracted with his phone in one hand and a burger in the other hand, using only his left knee to steer. When the driver looked up and noticed Rich in the middle of the road, he blared on the horn and tried to swerve out of the way, but Rich knew it was too late and dove behind a metal dumpster. The tractor trailer plowed right through the Subaru and shredded the car to pieces. Debris flew in all directions and the tractor trailer continued along, dragging one of the Subaru's rim plates under its back tire.

Rich peeked out behind the dumpster with his jaw hung open in disbelief. Everything he owned was now pulverized. *Thank heavens I am safe*, he thought, trying to stay in good spirits.

Rich had no choice after that moment but to sleep under parked cars, as his ego was too big to stay in a shelter. And he scoured the streets for edible scraps for weeks. Everyday he walked forty blocks to the Court Street soup kitchen near St. Philip's church because they served warm food every evening, and instead of staying at the homeless shelter at the church he'd walk back to the freight train depot at night. Because after ten years of marriage he needed his peace and quiet.

But on Saturdays he'd hang out at the soup kitchen with other homeless men, and drink 40 ounce bottles with them. They'd laugh about life and its brevity, each had their own story of how they'd come on hard times. But each day got better.

Rich ate the other half of his banana which he hoped would settle his rumbling stomach, but it didn't, so he bit into his overripe apple while admiring the beautiful colors patterned along the New York City skyline just across the Hudson river. *This is peaceful, and I am grateful for another day to live*, he thought. Rich pondered a better life, and a full stomach, recalling the old times when he made fast money on the streets, pushing the *grisly* for the infamous Marshall Steppe, who was recently killed in San Antonio by his brother Xavier. A family business deal went sour.

Rich lived in unfortunate circumstances, but still held his head high. And as he was just about ready to rest for the night, he heard a rustling sound. He turned and noticed a man approaching in the shadows.

II

Rich, partially weak, shivered as the man approached, his dim outline almost clear.

"Richard Prospere of all the places. Good to see you!" Sir Penn stood tall, his broad shoulders were prominent under his ripped shirt. He sold drugs with Rich years ago and lived the Tri-City motto: *Once a friend, always a friend.* "It's been ages!" They shook hands.

"I can't believe it's the Notorious S&P, of all people! I heard a rumor that you were still alive." Rich said, wiping the sweat off his brow.

"I've been walking all day." Sir Penn sat down on a piece of scrap wood in the freight train depot to catch his breath..

"What a day it's been," Rich said as his heart calmed down.

"How long have you been out here?" Penn asked, tilting his head to crack his neck bone. "You don't live in Roselle anymore?"

"Nah, Nancy's got the house. She caught me with my ex, Caitlin Fernwood… One of those afternoon days where one martini by the pool turned into Caitlin losing her bikini."

Sir Penn shook his head, sympathetically, staring at Rich unsure of how to respond.

"What are you staring at?" Rich asked.

"Sorry, you went through all that. You look like you're in good spirits though."

"Guess that's what divorce will do to ya. Put a smile right on your face." Rich laughed under his breath. "So what brings you out here Penn? This isn't a place to be roaming at night."

"Apparently not. But what if I told you that I need to sneak into Brick City, can you help me?" Sir Penn asked.

"No honestly. Ever since that mob burned down Xavier's home they've tightened the borders." Rich replied.

"But there's gotta be another way." Sir Penn said, recalling when Alin drove through a narrow passageway on the way to Frazier's mansion.

"I've lived on these streets for four months. If there was a secret way into Brick City, I'd know about it."

Penn felt adamant. "No! No! There must be, because I've seen it! It's a concrete wall that opens enough to let a small car through. If you don't know, I'll find it on my own."

Rich prickled his beard hair in deep contemplation. He couldn't let an old friend down, his heart would never allow it. "Hmmm. Now that you mention it, Penn. I'm thinking about Walden… There's a dead end street that ends at a concrete wall near the playground. I've heard about a lot of night activities going on over there but I've never seen it up close."

"Yeah you're on to something… Walden sounds familiar. That's gotta be it." Penn got up from the piece of lumber he was sitting on and pulled a splinter out of his ass.

III

"I'll lead the way." Rich said.

"I was hoping you would."

"Maybe we'll find some women." Rich said, smiling. He stood up tall and pulled his shoulders back.

"But Nancy might want you back? Ever thought of that?" Sir Penn asked.

"Ahhh she'd never trust me again. I saw it in her face that day when I left the house. And she probably has another guy already."

"But you're the man in the relationship. You should set the tone." Sir Penn hoped to rekindle the flame of his friend's marriage, but all Rich wanted was freedom and respect which he never received at home.

"Thanks for your confidence. But I'm starting a new chapter in my life… And you know buddy. If Nancy and I had gotten counseling before getting married, we probably wouldn't have been a match now that I look back on it." His voice grew somber. "She made sure to put me down for every little mistake. Then we'd argue all night. I don't think I even got a decent night's sleep our entire ten years of marriage. It was all her fault."

"Did you think she was happy?"

"I don't know. But marriage took a toll on me, Penn… She crippled my spirit and told me all these years I ain't worth more than hair off a cat's back." He paused. "Honestly, I haven't told a soul that story since I've been out here. But it does feel good getting it off my chest."

Sir Penn nodded, "sometimes that's all you need."

Richard Prospere set his satchel onto the ground and scoured through it one more time. "Just about ready, Penn. Oh shit! I forgot I have a blanket stashed around the corner and another set of clothes, give me a minute, I'll grab it."

"Sure thing." Sir Penn turned his face up to the starry night sky, the picturesque atmosphere of the Earth. The dark forms of clouds swirled, as he gazed at the heavens, feeling the intensity of the world around him. He snapped out his daydream when he heard Rich rounding the corner with a blanket and a set of clothes in his hands. Rich finished packing up his satchel and they both started walking together. Rich felt grateful to be hanging with an old buddy.

"Thanks for coming and picking up my spirits. I was getting lonely. Even though I love the quiet and I can see the stars."

As they walked through the dark streets in the Industrial section of the Tri-Cities, none of the businesses were open, except for a nightclub, open twenty four hours a day seven days a week. They were three blocks away from the club, where the partying never stopped, and could already hear the loud music.

They saw the spinning record shaped sign that said 'CLUB TANGO' in flashing LED lights. The club was once an old car dealership and renovated five years ago to be a fully nude nightclub. And it's thrived ever since. The music was loud and the people were louder. Luckily, there were no residential properties within a two mile radius.

"¡Oye amigos!" A group of drunk Spanish men yell over, seeing Penn and Rich walking closer.

"No stopping, let's keep moving," Penn said, then he noticed a shadow at the upcoming corner. "Do you see that up ahead? Looks like a woman."

IV

They walked closer and now heard the woman shouting over the phone. "You piece of shit! I'm outside Tango's. You said you'd pick me up. What the hell?" The street lamp above her flickered and burst at the treble of the speakers from Club Tango. "You're a douchebag Eddy! I'm done with you. I'm serious, leave me alone! D-O-N-E. Done." She pulled the phone away and stuffed it into her pocket.

Sir Penn whispered. "Let's go another way, Rich."

"No come on, we're almost there. There's a shortcut up ahead. Or else we'd have to go back the other way."

The two of them walked up to the street corner where the woman stood, fuming and stamping her feet. Her nerves stood up seeing them approach. She pulled out a large swiss army knife from her purse and pointed it at them. "You motherfucker! I'm gonna kill you right here." They stopped in their tracks. "Good thing you're not dead. I'd love to be the one to finish you off."

"What! I believe you've mistaken me for someone else." Penn screamed.

"There's no mistake! You killed my husband! It was you and I'll never forgive you." She charged at Sir Penn with the knife. Penn lunged away from her.

Rich stuck his leg out which caused her to trip and fall onto the pavement. "Not so fast." He said as she scraped her hands and elbows, and ripped her jeans. And her switchblade fell into a sewer grate.

"Fuck the both of you." She shouted helplessly on the floor, as Rich interlocked his arms around her in a stranglehold. She attempted to wrestle free but was unable.

"Let her loose bud," Sir Penn said.

"Why? She's manic."

"I said let her loose." Rich released his grip on her. She fell onto the pavement, fuming, crinkling her nose and rolling her eyes at them. "Why did you do it?" She yelled with tears pouring down her face. "Why did you kill my husband?"

"Although Marshall poisoned me with the *grisly* and left me for dead, I didn't kill him, it was someone else."

"Bullshit. We picked you up that morning," she wiped tears off her face, and continued. "Remember we went to that cafe and met up with Zechariah? Well that was the last time I ever saw him."

"I told you Marshall poisoned me with the *grisly*, right after he left the Tri-cities with the diamonds."

"You're a liar." She stared in detest.

"I'm sorry for all the pain and struggles you've been through Roxy, but it's true.."

"Can I ask you something?" Her eyes constricted.

"Sure." Sir Penn nodded.

"Was he sleeping with Caitlin? Please tell me he wasn't." Penn shook his head, not wanting to hurt her anymore.

"You know what makes me even more pissed at you Sir Penis." Roxy said. "The news reporters on TV and in the newspapers said you were part of the robbery, yet I still see you here, walking free when you should be in jail!"

"I didn't have anything to do with the robbery. Although I am part of the aftermath." Penn shrugged his shoulders. "You can believe whatever you want."

V

It was foggy and approaching midnight. Rich looked down the street and watched more street lights bursting at the sound of the club music. "There's a cop car approaching." He pointed out, but it was too late. "Oh shit! He saw us. Play it cool." Rich backed away from the group.

"If the cop asks my name is Ernest," Penn said.

"Ernest Hemingway! You always were a masochist." She yelled.

The red and blue lights flashed and the sirens wailed down the street, until the cop car parked in front of where the three of them hung suspiciously on the dark corner. The cop rolled down his window, his tan, thin and freckled face scanned them. He had a radio clipped to his pristine uniform.

"There's no loitering around these parts, and the new law says I can lock you up for being homeless. Get out of here." The cop was rolling up his window to let them go when Roxy interjected.

"Hey officer, today's your lucky day!" She said, waving a stubby finger at Penn. "Right there is Sir Sophus Penn! He's a *grisly* addict. And that's his friend." She pointed to Rich.

The cop snatched his radio from his collar, "Attention Precinct 234AS." He said, "We have a situation by Tango! Sir Sophus Penn, the *grisly* addict, is here along with two other suspects. Calling for backup. Meanwhile I will detain the subjects. Over." The officer jumped out of the car, and pulled his gun out. "You sleazy motherfucker." He aimed the gun right in Sir Penn's face. "Sergeant had me on duty for sixteen hours looking for you. You're apparently the most popular *grisly* addict that ever lived." The cop motioned closer, now on the sidewalk five yards from them. "I'll be the hero today, Penn, and I'll bring you to the Precinct in a bodybag. I'll show the precinct that I'm the new big shot in town."

Rich saw a window of opportunity and tossed his satchel at the cop, which caused the officer to stumble on the sidewalk and fall to the ground. The cop shot his gun from the ground, barely missing Rich who jumped behind a street bench just in time.

"Run!" Rich yelped. Penn hid on the other side of the cop car.

Roxy leaped at Sir Penn, grabbed him and clutched his shirt. "I want compensation for this officer," she yelled.

"Get off of him! Or I'll shoot you both!" The cop regained his composure now and was aiming for a good shot at Sir Penn. Then Rich ran from behind the bench and blindsided the cop and dropped him to the ground. Rich reached for the cop's gun but couldn't as they wrestled and rolled from side to side. The cop shot blindly a couple times, and one stray bullet hit Roxy in the shoulder.

"Ahhhhhhh." She screamed.

"Ay amigos, espera!" A group of three Spanish men who were hanging outside of Club Tango now ran towards them.

"I always wanted to hit an officer." One man said with a heavy Spanish accent. "And break all his ribs." He was serious. Two of the men pulled the cop off the sidewalk. And the larger of the three started swinging punches right at the cop's gut, like a ragdoll getting pummeled. "That'll teach you for locking up my amigos in Rikers Isle. I've been waiting for today, puta."

"Uh." The cop grunted.

"Rrrrrr. Rrrrrr." An assembly of cop cars head down the desolate street towards them. Their bright lights illuminating the dimly lit street.

"Hector, Silva! Let's go!" The three Spanish men ran back inside the club to hide in the bathroom stalls.

Meanwhile, Roxy laid on the floor, with blood gushing from her shoulder. Penn looked at her.

"Come on Penn! She'll be okay." They both ran across the street, as the sirens grew louder.

Roxy held out her arm and screamed, "I'll find you, and I'll make sure I kill you next time! Mark my words."

Penn followed Rich into a gloomy parking lot. They came up to a tall fence, "This is a shortcut over to Walden. We need to climb this fence, come on!" Rich climbed up like an acrobat and scaled down the other side, "I swear I'm too old for this!" Rich said, panting.

Sir Penn clutched the metal fence fiercely, climbing the grating but halfway up he slashed his hand, lost his grip and landed where he started. "Damn it, hurry up!" Rich cried out as police sirens approached.

"Coming." Sir Penn clutched the fence again, and climbed, despite his hands bleeding; adrenaline fueled him beyond all pain. He tapped into an inner strength that had never forsaken him. He ascended to the top of the fence, just as four cop cars pulled into the parking lot wailing their police sirens.

The headlights of the four cars saw them clearly. And the Captain of Police hopped out to scream, "Get down Penn we got you cornered!" Sir Penn closed his eyes and jumped ten feet down into a rolling landing, and then laid flat in the dirt. "You're going away for a long while. You too Richard Prospere!" He screamed.

Penn and Rich closed their eyes, hearing gunfire from all directions. They assumed the cops were firing at them. But after ten seconds they looked up and noticed a vigilante street gang on the opposite end of the parking lot shooting at the cops. One of them shouted in a harsh smoker's voice, "Hey Captain you're in our territory! If you bring me and my buddies a couple bags of the *grisly,* we'll leave you alone for the night."

"You lousy addicts! I can't wait to see you all dead on the side of the road. Give 'em hell men!" The Police Captain screamed back.

The vigilante group tossed a few Molotov cocktails one after another. The first two hit a police car which instantly roared in flames. Then the third hit the Captain's car, causing a group of officers to run out of the parking lot into the street, in the nick of time, before the two cars exploded.

"One last chance! I want a hand delivery of the finest *grisly* money can buy!"

"Fuck off! We got back up on the way."

Sir Penn and Rich looked at each other on the floor. "Now's our chance to sneak away."

VI

Rich led the way down a grim dirt road where crows were feasting on carcasses of dead raccoons.

"Rich. How far are we from Walden?"

"It's just up ahead."

They struggled the last half a mile until they made it to a vantage point in a park that had a good view of the Walden school.

"Hey Penn there's something going on down there. Check it out." Rich saw a headlight in the distance. "Do you see that?"

"Yeah, let's get closer." They walked towards the taillights of a car, idling next to the large concrete stone slab, just beyond the edge of the small park. They creeped up to the street beside the car, then saw the concrete wall open magnificently, a modern engineering marvel, opening a narrow path just wide enough for one car. The car drove in slowly.

"There's somebody watching." Rich whispered, pointing up to a man standing on top of a nearby building, pacing back and forth with an assault rifle between his hands.

"Wait til he turns the other way and we'll make a run for it." Sir Penn said.

"Are you crazy?!"

"Let's go! Now's our chance." Penn started running, and Rich tailed him. The guard saw the motion out of his peripheral vision and fired his rifle in their direction, missing them by inches.

They entered the passageway, which now started to close in on them. The car that had driven through already disappeared.

With only ten feet left to the other side, they ran faster than they ever had in their life. Penn screamed, "Jummmmmmp!" They both jumped; the wall closed; and they landed on a sidewalk in Brick City.

"Well, that's enough excitement for me." Rich remarked.

VII

Rich was unsure how he had landed in this predicament. He was happy to be with an old friend, but he wasn't happy to be damn near close to death already more than once in a few hours. "You weren't kidding before when you said it was a rough mission."

"Not one bit. You're risking a lot hanging with me pal." Sir Penn pointed out.

"You couldn't have said that any better."

"Let's keep moving." Sir Penn said as the first glimmer of sunlight peered beyond the horizon between the tall buildings. Ahead of them, three men lay slumped over, wasted on the sidewalk. Sir Penn approached them and put a $20 bill in each of their hands.

Sir Penn and Rich continued on Gerard St. and turned right on Burline Ave, where the neighborhood went from bad to worse, making the Industrial section of the Tri-Cities look like the Diamond District. Along both sides of this street were brick buildings, all pathetically rundown with wooden planks boarded up across every window. Sir Penn stopped in his tracks.

"What's going on bud," Rich turned to ask.

"Do you see what I'm seeing?" Penn stared at a grotesque building, which seemed to blend in, but something about it was different. "Looks just as bad as all the rest." Rich said.

"Yeah but look at that." He pointed at the driveway. "Why is there a passenger van parked there with blacked out windows?"

"I don't know Penn, but I don't think we should get caught up in this. The rest of the building is boarded up like all the others."

"Yeah but look at that graffiti." They stared at a huge mural of a leviathan painted on the side of the wall. Penn knew there was a Brick City gangster called the Leviathan AKA The Creep. He got a chill going down his spine.

"We may have found The Creep's underground operation."

"Give me a break, Penn. Even if we did, you can't convince me to walk in there with you. If its really him, this is suicide."

"I won't let something like this go down on my watch. Let's go in."

"Nah it's boarded up."

"There's gotta be another way in." Penn walked to the side of the building, "I know there's a door here." He felt the bricks along the wall.

"Now you've lost it, " Rich said.

"Ha! Here we go." Sir Penn found a groove in the graffiti just under the leviathan's tail. He pulled it and a small door opened. They both stepped into a dark hallway.

"Where's the lightswitch?"

"I can't find it!" Sir Penn felt around. "Ohh wait, I got it."

Click. A bulb fizzled above them inside an old fluorescent fixture, swinging ominously back and forth. They were on a small landing where one flight of steps led upstairs to a blue door and one flight of steps led downstairs to a red door.

"I'll take the upstairs. You take the bottom Rich."

"I can't believe you got me into this." Rich said.

Penn started walking up the steps. "Go ahead bro, you'll be safe." Penn reached the top of the landing and attempted to open the door but it was locked. He knocked and waited.

. . .

Rich opened the red door and noticed a line of workers standing alongside heavy machinery used for metal moldings. The workers were arrayed in rows, like an assembly line, fastening metals of various shapes. They each wore thick coverall suits to protect themselves from molten debris, which splayed every time the machines were used. Rich couldn't believe these conditions. "Hey!" He yelled. "Everybody out!" A few of the workers looked up from their posts but continued with their work. He ducked, almost getting hit by a flying molten shard then he yelled again, "I said everybody out!" Nobody paid him any attention.

He looked around and saw a fire alarm in the back of the room. He motioned across the floor, fearful for his life but still made his way to press the alarm, which caused the emergency sirens to go off. "Get out of here!" He screamed. Then he heard banging on a door in the back. He opened the door and more workers in suits ran out.

"Ay dios mio!" He heard them yell frantically.

"Wait!" Another voice said. "There's no emergency, we should wait!"

"I will run." Said a woman in broken English. "Even one minute from here would be heaven."

"Yes!" Another voice said.

"Everybody out!" Rich yelled as the workers hurried to the door. Then a gunshot went off, piercing over the fire alarm. as a man in a biker's jacket came into the room, carrying an assault rifle. Rich hid behind one of the industrial machines. "Who pulled the fire alarm?" The man asked. All the workers froze and pointed behind the machine at Rich.

"Get your ass out from behind there. I'm taking you upstairs." The man in the biker jacket said, first going to the fire alarm panel to turn off the siren.

Rich crawled out from behind the machine and walked forward up to the man in the biker jacket, who forcibly grabbed Rich's wrist and twisted it. "ARRGGGHHH!" Rich whimpered on the floor, holding his arm.

"Come on! Move!" The man poked him in the ass with his gun and beckoned him to walk towards the door. Rich made his way, one step at a time until he was at the blue door at the top of the staircase.

VIII

The man with the biker jacket swung the blue door open on the upper landing.

"Get in there!" He shoved Rich onto a large warehouse floor. Three men stood around a chair in the middle of the room where Sir Penn sat restrained by a rope, his face helpless.

The man in the biker jacket hit Rich over the head with the backside of the gun and Rich fell onto his face, unconscious. "Good job Flex, handling that situation down there." Said a short, stubby man, called Donald Eddy or better known as The Creep, head of an underground metal factory that incorporated underage children as slaves. The Creep was 5"2', at least sixty years old, with the face of a bulldog but still with a full head of hair. He had his shoulders slumped back and a tattoo on his arm of a leviathan, a smaller version of the one outside the building.

The Creep punched Sir Penn in the chest. "I'm gonna torture you for being a meddler and showing up unannounced! Nobody dares sabotage my operations." He unleashed punches one after another like a professional boxer.

"Boss! Give him a breather! Or his kidney will come up his throat." A skinny man to the right said. He looked pinheaded and had stubble on his face, his eyes were disfigured, one larger than the other.

"Shut up Inbred!" The Creep said in response. Then he turned to Flex. "Flex, is the accomplice still breathing?"

Flex bent down to check Rich's pulse. "Yes boss."

"Okay leave him for now he looks battered." Rich laid there unconscious with his arms flailed about and a hematoma growing on his head.

"Who are these guys?" Flex asked.

"They're a bunch of low-lifes from the Tri-Cities. Old *grisly* salesmen from years ago." The Creep gave one more punch into Sir Penn's stomach, this time Penn coughed up a lot of blood.

"Told you Boss! You gave it to him mighty good. Too good if you want him to live."

"Cut it Inbred! You and Mute go and stand over in the corner. Shut up and wait for my instructions."

"You know I don't like that name boss."

"Fuck what you like, it's either Inbred or Pansy! Which do you prefer? I'd ask Mute but I know he'll back me up." Mute was about the same height as The Creep, but had tattoos all over his body. Tattoos of skulls, cemetery plots and the grim reaper. Even Mute's eyeballs were tattooed with skulls in them. He looked so scary everyone called him Mute. He needn't ever say anything to get his way.

"Why can't you call me by my real name?" Inbred said, with his face looking more deformed in the light, his larger eye looked like it grew.

"Maybe I would if you earned my respect! Now shut up and take notes!" The Creep growled and twitched his nose to the side, letting off a ruthless fart. He smiled as Inbred and Mute backed away and stood to the side of the room. "Flex, I don't hear those machines running. Do me another favor and go back downstairs and make sure everyone is back to work."

"Yes boss." Flex made his way back down the steps with his gun slung over his shoulder.

Sir Penn spit up a wad of blood from his mouth and it landed right in front of The Creep's gray suede shoes, the blood splattered and stained the front brim.

"Why, you lousy…" The Creep winded an arm back to strike but before he could, Sir Penn blurted out. "You know Mr. Frazier never lets go of a grudge!" The Creep retracted his arm in shock.

"Frazier's got eyes and ears all over the streets." Sir Penn said, doing whatever it took to stay alive. He relied on his intuition, knowing he could work his way out of this jam. Self-Preservation is the strongest human instinct.

"He still holds that stupid grudge, it's been over six years since I left the Tri-Cities." The Creep turned and looked around the room, thinking, *if Mr. Frazier sent Sir Penn then I'm in trouble for beating the shit out of him.*

"Can you tell me anything about the Plaza? Anything going on there, relatively soon?" The Creep spun on one heel, smooth for a big guy. He was the sole owner of the Plaza hotel, and possibly knew about Xavier's whereabouts.

"What's Frazier want? Money?" He choked on his words, and his face twitched unconsciously.

"I'm only the messenger," Sir Penn said.

"Frazier doesn't give a shit about my racket. Cut your bullshit! I'm gonna sink your teeth into the floor tile."

"Maybe this'll all go by the wayside if you give me info on the Plaza."

"No need. I'll have Flex do the honors to knock your brains loose when he comes back up." In response, Penn spit more blood at The Creep, who stepped back far enough this time.

Flex re-entered the room with a young teenage girl walking in front of him, her hands on her head. She hesitated. "I said move." He pointed the assault rifle at her head. Then she cried and showed her torn and weathered face. "I caught her trying to smash through the window downstairs. She almost escaped too."

"You naughty girl, you're gonna have to pay for that." The Creep said. She lifted her head and looked at him, but her eyes cowered from the light. She hesitated again, this time Flex pushed her down onto her hands and knees. And The Creep stared at her while she was on the floor. "How pleasant it is to see you in your natural position." He said, before Flex grabbed her by the back of her shirt and brought her to her feet. "Flex, lock her in my office. How's the rest of the operation look downstairs?"

"Everyone else is back to work, with no loss of production time." Flex opened the office door and pushed the teenager inside. "Sit on the chair over there and be quiet." He closed the door and locked it from the outside. He stepped over Rich, who was still unconscious, then to the center of the room.

"Excellent." The Creep said. "And for your good service Flex I want to increase your ranking level in the Brick City underground, since I know you've been asking for a promotion lately. Well here's your chance. All you need to do is kill this fucker. Any last words Sir Penn?"

"Flex," Sir Penn said. "Don't listen to this creep. He wants you to kill me so his ass is covered. But you better believe that Mr. Frazier's gonna be after you if you kill me."

Meanwhile, Mute and Inbred were looking out of the tinted warehouse window, watching a group of rats in an alleyway fighting over a sliver of pizza. The largest rat won the standoff and dragged the pizza into the side alley of the building. This made them roar out laughing.

IX

Sir Penn looked over at Rich, who was conscious now. They winked at each other. *It's now or never.*

Penn used his weight to swing side to side in the chair until it tipped over as Rich crawled his way forward to knife Flex in the shin. Flex screamed in agony and fell to the ground. Mute and Inbred heard the commotion and turned around wielding their guns, but they were too late because Rich lunged for Flex's assault rifle and shot madly at them both. They fell like a ton of bricks.

Thud. Thud. "Game over suckas." Rich said, standing up straight now and pointing the gun at The Creep. "Get down!."

"Nice job Rich. Now get me untangled here."

Rich held the gun as he untied the rope, freeing Sir Penn. From the corner of his eye Rich saw The Creep slither on the floor.

"Be careful of your next move." The Creep stopped and Sir Penn grabbed the rope to wrap it around Donald Eddy, The Creep.

"I'll kill you for this Penn!" The Creep yelled.

"Anything going on over at the Plaza Hotel? If you want to live you better talk!" The Creep remained silent.

Rich pointed the gun at The Creep's head.

"Ok! Ok! Xavier! He's meeting me at the Plaza."

"When?"

"I don't know."

"You have one more chance." Sir Penn said standing over him.

"I'm done talking to you. Call Mr. Frazier." The Creep said.

"I thought you'd never ask." Sir Penn pulled out the burner phone that Stephen gave him before he left Frazier's mansion yesterday.

"Yeah go ahead." Frazier answered over speakerphone.

"It's Penn, calling in an update."

"Well this better be good. I got two chinese women on me like chop suey."

"Looks like Xavier is meeting Donald Eddy at the Plaza Hotel in Brick City."

"No chance! The Creep couldn't be that stupid."

"He is because I have him tied up right in front of me."

"Damn this is good! Excellent work Penn. I knew you were the right man for the job." Mr. Frazier remarked.

"Hey Frazier," The Creep began. "Looks like your men have caught me in a pickle."

"Well, think of it this way. If you don't talk I'll make sure that pickle gets shoved up your ass."

"There was a small deal that came across my desk over the weekend. However, I'm not obliged to say anything about it."

"Penn!" Frazier screamed on the phone. "Make sure you beat this guy's ass really good, for wasting my time."

"Give me the word and I'll put the bullet right through his thick skull. We'd be doing the world a favor. He's got a bunch of underage kids working in his metal shop downstairs."

"Hold it! Hold it!" The Creep squirmed. "I'll tell you everything! Just please, let me keep my business."

"Well hurry up and start talking! These Chinese women want some action and I'm not a young stud anymore." Mr. Frazier relayed.

"All I know is that Xavier is looking to sell his share of the diamonds. He says they're cursed and no one else is willing to get mixed up with him. But I don't believe any of that. One thing you'll never catch me being is superstitious. All I know is it's a deal of a lifetime. For once I'm a lucky man."

"How much does he want?"

"1 million."

"He's desperate, diamonds of that quality are worth ten times that amount. Easily!" Frazier said.

"Exactly! That's why he had a hard time selling. Nobody trusts him either. But anyhow I have plans for these diamonds. I want to give them to my girls. They deserve something nice for their hard work." He gave a perverted look towards his office door, where the teenage girl Brenda was locked in. "And the rest are for keepsakes."

Rich knocked The Creep in the face with the gun, giving him a nice gash on the side of his face. "That's for being a dirtbag."

Frazier began. "If you cooperate with us I'll let you keep the diamonds and the money. When are you meeting him?"

"7PM tomorrow outside the Plaza."

"I'll have my men over there."

"This might be a trap." Penn interjected, remembering that Selah spoke with Xavier on the phone yesterday. Something didn't add up. Silence. Then a playful sound in the background.

"Sorry. Yuka and Ruka are fiddling with my head a little bit. Hey, cut it out!" He pulled the phone away. "What's your location? I'll send some men over now to keep an eye on The Creep."

Then the call disconnected. Sir Penn attempted to call back but the lines were busy. He looked over at Donald Eddy, the man who had done unthinkable things to countless children. Penn couldn't stop his anger. "You're fucking lucky you're still living Creep!" Sir Penn said as he wriggled out the key ring from Flex's pockets in order to open the office door. The girl Brenda ran out crying.

"If you touch her I'll kill you!" The Creep yelled from across the room.

"Shut up!" Penn screamed. Rich kneaded the gun into The Creep's cheekbone again.

"Rich, take that gun downstairs and tell everyone that they better leave now."

"What about Flex? He's still alive. Should we leave him there?" Rich asked.

"Yeah he won't get far."

X

Rich stared into The Creep's eyes. "You fucking piece of shit!" He swung the gun into his face one more time and knocked a couple of his teeth out. But The Creep still had a perverse smile. "You deserve more, but that'll do for now!" Rich headed down the stairs.

Sir Penn took the young girl in his arms and they walked out of the building. "It's okay. You'll be safe. Everything will be okay," he tried to tell her.

"No. It's not safe here!" She said in a Slovakian accent.

"But you're away from the bad man in there."

"No!" she screamed. "The other men will find me. I know they will!"

"Who'll find you!" She was silent. Sir Penn kneeled down and gripped her shoulders. "Tell me so I can help!" He shook her while tears poured down her face.

Rich stepped out of the building followed by seventy workers, who ran wildly down the street in their white jumpsuits. Brenda squeezed free from Sir Penn's grip and followed the others.

"I hope you know what you're doing, Penn." Rich said, doubting his friend.

"You'll have to trust me. Have faith Rich!" The sun shone brightly onto the street, and Rich had a miserable look on his face. Sir Penn realized he dragged Rich into something larger than he could handle. "Dammit Rich! Let's follow the workers. I know someone will talk! And throw that gun in the bushes! What are you crazy?"

Rich tossed the gun.

"Stop Penn! We can't chase them!" He cried out.

"What if there's more operations like this? Or even worse?" Penn yelled, seeing the group stopped up ahead, beside the major highway Route 1 & 9. He saw them look both ways about ready to run for it. "WAITTTT!!!" Penn screamed, running up to them from behind.

The group of runaway slave workers made haste and sprinted across the highway as cars flew by going fifty to sixty miles per hour in both directions. All the cars slammed on their horns and a large truck screeched on its brakes, swerving into the next lane, barely missing them. Penn's heart raced. "Oh my God!" Then the truck overturned and blocked the entire Southbound roadway.

The workers made it across, weaving in and out of the oncoming lanes. Every car on the highway came to a halt and people screamed out their window because of the gore of the dead bodies on the road.

"Come on Rich! We can still follow them." Penn said.

"Are you trying to get us both killed?" Rich ran as his physical body deteriorated and his spirit was to follow suit next.

Penn continued running and Rich lagged behind again.

"Rich! Come on!" Penn approached a large gathering of people who were watching the commotion on the highway.

XI

"Over here!" Penn heard a young Middle-Eastern man in a business suit shouting towards him.

"Who are you?" Penn stopped and asked.

"Haseem, you don't remember me?"

"Do I know you from somewhere?" Penn said.

Rich caught up to them now, panting, and out of the corner of his eye noticed a suspicious van driving down the side street Burline Ave closer to them. "Penn, we should keep moving." He said.

"Hold on Rich." Penn brushed him off. " I apologize for my friend. But we have been on a tormentous adventure and should keep moving." Penn stretched his arm out and gave Haseem a handshake.

"Farewell Sir. I shall see you in due time." Haseem had a deceitful grin on his face, and gripped Sir Penn tightly in the handshake for a prolonged period. Penn attempted to pull out his hand, forcibly, when a large cargo van pulled up to the curb in front of them. The side door opened. Penn froze in shock, seeing two men in face masks jump out, snatch him, and pull him into the van.

"Good work Haseem." One of the men said while the other man pulled out two pairs of handcuffs and cuffed Sir Penn's arms then feet.

Rich began sprinting; he raced across the highway and hopped the median.

"Should we get him?" One of the men in the van asked Haseem.

"Forget about him. He's a street rat."

"Well get in Haseem. We need to move now."

"No. The doctor wants me to meet him at his office in the Tri-Cities. You go ahead." Haseem said.

They nodded, closed the side door of the van and drove off down the highway.

Haseem noticed the crowd of people at the bus stop eyeing him. "What are you staring at! Get back to playing word puzzles on your phones!" He yelled. They were petrified.

Mostly everyone turned their attention away from Haseem, except one older man who sat on the bench of the bus stop. "You know you're going to pay for that!" He called out to Haseem.

"What did you say grandpa? Grow a sack of balls and look away!"

The man stood up defiant. "I said you're going to pay for that!" The crowd stared again.

"Who the fuck do you think you are?" Haseem asked.

"My name is Zechariah Von Barstool. And you can do anything you want to me but rest assured that by betraying that man Sir Penn you will be compensated in the worst way!"

"Listen drunkard! I know who you are.. You're a bum, a beggar, a nobody! You have nothing. I look down on you with contempt. You're an addict. And you've accomplished nothing but self-defeat. Don't stamp your pompous shit on me." He pushed Zechariah to the floor. Everybody gasped. The old man struggled to get up. "Today is a glorious day! The day I became rich!" Haseem shouted just as a large city bus screeched up to the bus stop and opened its doors, and a few passengers came out.

Within seconds Haseem ran inside the bus, pulled a pistol out from his pocket, and waved it at all the people sitting. He shouted, "Everybody out! This is a solo ride!" The passengers obeyed and shimmied down the aisle to exit.

XII

"I want a straight ride into the Tri-Cities. Better start moving." Haseem said, putting his pistol to the driver's head.

"But Mr... every vehicle must be searched upon entering the Tri-Cities."

"Well you're gonna have to come up with a good story to get around that one then!"

"Yes Mr." The man started driving, his hands were trembling and Haseem sat in the first aisle behind him, keeping the gun pointed at the driver as he drove. Soon the driver's face looked like Niagara Falls; he had pit stains developing under his armpits and his ass.

"Can you speed up this gravy train! I'm on a tight schedule."

"Yes Mr." The driver accelerated, and swerved in and out of lanes, cutting off several cars. He ran the next red light and bashed into a hot dog stand that was crossing the road, the owner fell back, unscathed, but hotdog buns flew everywhere. "Hey! Who taught you to drive!?" The hotdog stand owner shouted.

"Keep moving, the exit is coming up." Haseem said.

"I hope you know what you're doing Mr." The driver said, driving down the exit ramp that said TRI-CITIES.

"If you question me again, you're gonna be talking with the angels. And stop fucking sweating so much!" The driver's face was drenched. A pool of sweat was accumulating under his feet. "What are you gonna say at the gate? You've had time to think it over."

The driver gulped and gathered his thoughts. "Well… I can say my daughter is about to have a baby at St. Elizabeth's hospital. She is expecting in a few months and she lives in the Tri-Cities, so it's not a total lie."

"Perfect! Go ahead." There was a large sign posted above the three main gates that read: BORDER CROSSING TO TRI-CITIES, but they were in a mile of traffic as only two of the gates were used for public access. The third gate was for special uses only, its lane was empty with another large sign above it that read AUXILIARY GATE: EMERGENCY USES ONLY.

"Go right up to that gate." Haseem said.

"We'll be cutting the line by two miles. I could get in a lot of trouble and possibly lose my CDL license."

"I don't give a damn! And you'll be a pool of blood if you don't listen to my orders. Stick with the story. Fucking do it!" Haseem screamed; then disappeared in the back of the bus, making sure to stay undetected. The driver slowly pulled towards the auxiliary gate. Some cars beeped their horns but the bus driver ignored them and kept moving, until he stopped in front of the partition for the patrol booth, where a border officer was stationed not paying any attention to anything beside his phone. The bus driver used this second to wipe the remaining sweat from his face.

"Come on! We don't have all day." Haseem said under his breath.

The officer finally looked up from his desk, startled to see a Brick City bus sitting at the emergency gate. He beckoned the bus to approach the window. The bus driver pulled up. "What's the issue? This lane is for authorized personnel only."

"Please officer. I threw all my passengers off because my daughter is going into labor any minute at St. Elizabeth's. This will be my first grandchild and I want to be in the waiting room to greet her newborn baby."

"That's not a credible emergency, unfortunately." The officer looked up at the sky, upset that this interfered with his movie. "But you know what though… I'm in a good mood. Give me your ID and I'll call this into the station, and see what they say. It's worth a shot." The bus driver handed over his ID. The officer scanned it.

"Okay Mr. Williams. How long have you been a bus driver?"

"17 years."

"And this is your correct address?"

"Yes 47 Malbec Road, Brick City, New Jersey." The driver began sweating profusely. "Sorry officer, I'm nervous as hell. And frantic. I don't think I can handle being a grandfather."

"Calm down. Give me a second. Let me call this in." The officer closed the window of the patrol booth and picked up the phone.

Haseem stayed quiet, hidden under one of the aisles in the back of the bus. He hoped they wouldn't do a police search of the vehicle. "What the hell is taking so long?" Haseem whispered, clutching the edge of his seat.

The cop hung up the phone, typed something into his computer screen, then opened his patrol booth window again. Mr. Williams stuck out his arm to take his ID back.

"You're all set. I made a call to my police chief and they are aware you are on your way. Please wait over to the shoulder and the chief himself will be giving you a personal escort to the hospital. He wants to go inside with you too when you get there."

"Thank you!"

"No worries, have a safe day." Mr. Williams drove over to the shoulder and waited.

"Fuck. Fuck!" Haseem cursed and punched the seat in front of him.

"What's wrong Mr?" The driver asked.

"What a ton of shit this is. Police escort… Give me a break."

"Hey, at least we made it to the Tri-Cities. Isn't that what you wanted?"

"Yeah but not like this." Haseem began. "Once you get to the throughway, I want you to slow down a bit so I can jump out the back door. Make sure you don't lose the Chief though. When you get to the hospital, tell him that you slowed down because of a cat crossing the road or something."

Haseem crawled towards the door in the back of the bus. "When I say to slow down, you slam the brakes!" Haseem looked at all the speeding cars, and almost had a change of heart. "It's not as easy as they make it look in the movies. But what the hell." Then he saw an empty flatbed truck entering the highway at the next ramp.

"Get over to the next lane." The driver followed the orders. The bus was in the lane next to the empty flatbed.

"Okay! Slow down! NOW!" The brakes on the bus screeched as Haseem flung open the emergency door, jumped out like a stunt double onto the empty flatbed, rolled over and held onto the chain hoist for dear life. In the next lane, the bus regained its speed and continued following the police chief. Haseem watched them drive on.

The bus driver knew he was in deep shit, but had no choice but to keep following the chief, until they made it to St. Elizabeth's hospital. There they both parked in front of the Main hospital entrance. The chief got out of his car first and stood beside the bus. The driver opened the door.

"What was that on the throughway? I almost lost you." The chief said. The bus driver sat there, shaking and quiet. "Everything alright Mr. Williams?"

Mr. Williams tensed up, thinking of his family. He had to tell the truth. "I illegally transported a man across the border. And he escaped out the backdoor when I slowed down before on the throughway."

Now furious, the chief of police pulled up Mr. Williams from his chair. "What! Are you serious?" Then he tossed the man onto the floor of the bus. "You may never go home to Brick City again. We have a special chamber here for slums like you."

"I swear that's all I know."

Mr. Williams was on the floor whimpering. "He had a gun on me, officer. Please spare me, I'm an old man. I just want to go home and be with my family."

"I don't give a rat's ass."

XIII

Haseem landed on the back of a flatbed truck. "Arghhhh!" He grabbed his shoulder in pain and rolled to his left, falling onto the side of the road. The truck driver heard a loud noise from behind but when he turned to look, Haseem had already rolled off, and the truck kept driving on. Haseem jumped up on the throughway, his shirt sleeve ripped, and a little gash bleeding near his shoulder. He ran off the highway towards Hearth Mill Street and struck an elderly woman who stopped at the corner to look down and check her purse. "Eeeyyyyaaahhh!" She screamed, tossed her arms up, as her glasses flew off her nose and she collapsed into the street.

Haseem kept running, making his way to 2nd Ave. Out of breath, he continued sprinting on sheer will and strength. He probably only had a few minutes 'til the police would be looking for him. He made it to a small building in Roselle, the sign out front said 'Private Practitioner Dr. Trevis.' He scaled the driveway and knocked on the side door, looking frantically both ways.

"Who is it?" A voice said over the intercom.

"It's Haseem. I have good news."

"Splendid! Just the person I was waiting to see. Come in! I'll be up in a minute." Click. An electronic latch disengaged and the door opened. Haseem walked into the dark building and sat on one of the sofas on his immediate left. The sofa was made of cheap plastic, about as rigid as stoneboard. He hurt his ass sitting on it too fast. He tried to move into a comfortable position but it was no use. He sat there patiently, took in a deep breath and smelled something foul in the air.

The walls in the waiting room were bare except for one photo of Dr. Trevis and his late wife Peggy. They were a picturesque couple but no one had ever seen them together in public. Apparently Peggy had an autoimmune disease and needed to stay indoors. And her husband tended to her for years. Then the poor woman died before her 39th birthday. Her body was shipped back to Nebraska to be with her family. No one thought anything about it and Dr. Trevis never mentioned it.

Metal bells rang in the hallway. The Doctor bent down to enter the doorway. He was a tall thin man, wearing a lab coat and goggles. "Hello Hachem," he pronounced Haseem's name wrong. Then two dogs entered the room and stood at the doctor's side. On the left of the doctor was a stocky gray bulldog as wide as long, with a menacing, slobbering mouth. And on his right was a large beige mastiff with muscular legs and its ears pointed up. The bulldog greeted Haseem by barking back manically. Haseem jumped out of his chair, "Woah! Who are your friends here?"

"Well the little guy is Bugsy." The doctor pointed at the bulldog, "and this young lady is Esta."

"Little guy?" Haseem responded. "Looks like he'd bite a baby's face off."

"Ah don't be a coward. Man up!" Dr. Trevis took off his goggles and let them hang on his neck. "I need these two by my side for protection, especially now that we're getting close."

Bugsy started barking again and Esta joined in the chorus. "Calm down. This is a friend of mine. He's harmless." The doctor looked down at the dogs and they stopped barking, but kept eyeing Haseem.

"Come." He motioned his arm. "Follow me downstairs. I want to talk more with you about our findings and what this means for humanity."

Haseem looked at the doctor and rubbed his thumb against his first two fingers, making sure he made his point. "Ah of course." The doctor nodded. "We will also be discussing compensation for your services."

Haseem proceeded forth behind the doctor and the two dogs, still glued to their master's side. The walls in the hallway had various medical diagrams displayed of the skeletal system, muscular system, and nervous system. Rich glanced at them in passing and watched the doctor open a door at the end of the hall revealing an old staircase loaded with cobwebs. Haseem now felt sick to his stomach, but continued in what looked to be a dingy basement with an open floor plan. In the center of the basement was a large operating table and an industrial sized sink, filled with beakers, droppers and utensils.

"Stay here." The doctor waved a finger at the two dogs, who waited near the steps. Then, he walked to the operating table and grabbed a box at the far right marked with the initials S.P. "Hey check this out." The doctor handed the box to Haseem.

"Should I open it?"

"It's not necessary" The doctor's eyes seemed to almost pop out of their sockets, he was so excited. "Right there in this box is brain fluid taken from Sir Penn's subconscious mind while he was in my custody at St. Elizabeth's hospital. As far as we know he is only one of the two men who have ever completely conquered the *grisly* addiction." The doctor paced back and forth, with his hands behind his back.

"By the *grisly*, you mean the street drug?"

"That's right. There have been many tests done on the *grisly* and the results are shocking; how it completely takes over all the neurons in the brain, it's easily the most addictive substance in the world. Only Sir Sophus Penn and Xavier Bonaparte have completely been cured of their addiction to the *grisly*."

"How were they able to overcome it?" Haseem asked.

"That is the most valuable question and I almost have my answer. I just need to run a few more tests. Please tell me Sir Penn is safe."

"He's safe and should be at the underground lab in Brick City."

"Okay, perfect. I must get there right away! There is a lot we must do before Detective Sordenburg brings in Xavier later tonight." Dr. Trevis patted Haseem on the back. "You don't know the service you have done for humanity Haseem."

"What's your next step after you run these tests tonight?" Haseem asked.

"It depends on how effective the antiserum is on our *two* prize subjects."

"What's the antiserum?"

"It's a drug I've created that is stronger than the *grisly*. But it's effective in taking out the spiritual side of humanity, essentially making them living zombies. I have a patent lawyer waiting to write up this discovery, and few people who are interested in the rights, especially the government."

"Woah! How much money are we talking about?"

"Your cut would be at least four and a half million. But there's one more thing Haseem, I'd like to discuss first."

"Of course. Anything! What's up?" Haseem asked.

"I don't think you understand how monumental this discovery is, and how much work I've put into this." He pointed both his thumbs at his chest, "And I don't really feel like sharing my profits with anyone."

"But Doc! We're a team. I've been indebted to you for over four years. And I believed in you even when your practice almost closed down."

The doctor walked up to Haseem, reached into his lab coat and pulled out a syringe and jabbed Haseem right in the neck. "I'm sorry Haseem. That it has to be this way." Haseem's face turned white immediately, his eyes widened. The box he was holding fell, the lid opened, and a bunch of confetti came out. Haseem fell over, shaking, helplessly. "You are the first subject injected with Sir Penn's subconscious fluid. How does it feel?" He pulled the syringe out of Haseem's neck. "Now let me give you the antiserum and see how you feel." Dr. Trevis pulled out a blue vial of liquid from his lab coat and filled another syringe with it. "This will only hurt a lot," he said, injecting the syringe this time into Haseem's upper thigh. Haseem started throwing up bile but his face regained color. "How does that feel?" the doctor asked.

"What did you do to me?" Haseem said with his mouth covered in pasty liquid.

"You're my first guinea pig. Now I have no use for you."

"What!"

"Dogs?" He looked over at his two compatriots; they were still barking over near the steps. "I promised you a full course meal. Ready to eat?" They hopped up and down. Then the doctor pulled Haseem by the collar. "How can you do this? We're partners." Haseem coughed up.

"Buenas Noches?" He said before tossing Haseem right in front of the two animals. They chewed Haseem's face off.

Dr. Trevis looked away and made a phone call. "Hey Gloves."

"Yeah doc."

"Tighten up security, there's no room for mishaps. The detective will be delivering Xavier any minute. I'll be right over." Click. Dr. Trevis grabbed a few of his belongings, brushed off the lab table, and walked past the dogs gnawing at Haseem's body.

"Great work guys. In case you're hungry later you can have the bones too... I gotta do something important." He walked up the creaky steps and back down the hall into the waiting room. He noticed a crooked picture frame, the one of him with his late wife Peggy. He centered it before exiting the front door.

XIV

Mr. Frazier pushed the two Chinese women to the side. "Sorry girls, we have to finish this later." They looked disappointed.

"But Mr. Frazier!" Yuka said, fully nude beside him.

"What about our weekly allowance? You said it would be double if we stay long." Ruka then stood up topless wearing jean shorts and her hair wrapped in a chopstick.

"There's an important matter I must attend to here. I'll be back later, you girls rinse off."

"No!" Yuka yelled. "We want our money now."

"You bitch!" Frazier slapped her across the face; she recoiled, and rolled off the couch, struggling up with a swollen cheek. She picked her clothes up in a bundle and ran out the room.

"You evil man!" Ruka screamed at him. "We'll be back, you asshole!" She kissed Frazier on the forehead then followed Yuka out the door.

Frazier yelled. "Call the home phone before you come back tonight! And you better bring Masiya I keep telling you."

Frazier, alone, picked up his phone and called Alin, who answered on the first ring.

"It's unlike you to call during your scheduled meeting times."

"Alin we have an issue in Brick City. Assemble the best men you can muster in short notice. And let them know this job is paying double."

"Boss, it's gonna be difficult. The news about Sparky is still fresh on everyone's mind."

"I don't give a damn. My reputation is on the line here Alin, don't fuck this up! In any case I'd settle for Poindexter and Ghost. They owe me anyway. Tell them they have no choice and this needs to happen fast. I have your bonus too and you'll get it after this job."

"I'm right on it."

"Gather the men and meet me in my study in half an hour…"

"You're joking, right? It's gonna take me half an hour just to drive there."

"Alright I'll give you forty five minutes. That'll give me time to shower and get ready. Now hurry!" Frazier hung up the phone, walked to his grand master bathroom, but before he closed the door he shouted down the stairs to his wife. "Helen!"

"What!" She screamed back. "Aren't you busy with your little girlfriends? I'm trying to make lasagna!"

"Have some food and coffee ready in my study in forty five minutes!" His boisterous voice shook the walls of the hallway. "I'm jumping in the shower. Alin will be here in a little bit."

"God damn Frazier! Why'd you give Stephen the day off? I've been slaving all day here!"

"He had to see his mother! She's ill!"

"Yeah I know. And whenever he sees his mother he comes back reeking of booze and pot smoke. He's a good liar. Didn't his mother die when he was a kid?"

"Shut up Helen. Just do as I say!" Frazier raised his voice and slammed the bathroom door. He rinsed off and dressed into a professional suit. He was about to go downstairs when his wife's beagle, Ginger, wobbled up to him on three legs, making a jingling noise with her bell collar. "Get out of here, you mutt!" He pushed the dog away forcefully. He hated that Ginger always came up to him whenever he put on clean clothes, then she'd try to jump on him and rip his pants. Rupf. Rupf. She barked playfully and looked at him in awe. "Not now!" He yelled back to the little creature.

Ding. The doorbell chime went off.

"Helen! The door!"

Part IV

I

"How ya doing back there champ? Feelin' alright?" The man in the passenger seat asked. Sir Penn tried to open his eyes but he was blindfolded.

"Hey Jonesy, Gloves know we're on our way?"

"Yeah of course."

"Just making sure. We can't afford any mishaps."

"Did you frisk him before cuffing him?"

"I thought you did!"

"Motherfucker! We've been partners for ten years and you still amaze me at your stupidity. Dean, pull over right here." The van stopped on the side of an empty road, no cars came in either direction.

"Guess I have to do everything. Like always." He roughly patted down Sir Penn, who stayed quiet.

"Ah! Look what you missed, Reno." He revealed a Motorola flip phone.

"Didn't even know they made those anymore!"

"Look how small that thing is!" Jonesy said. "It'd fit right in his pussy!" They started roaring.

Sir Penn spoke for the first time since getting captured. "Well, I'll shove it up the three of your pussies when I get the chance!" Jonesy gave Sir Penn an elbow shot to the ribs as the van rocked heavily, continuing down the road.

"Damn suspension!" Dean, the driver said, braking abruptly in the middle of the street. Everyone jerked forward.

"What the hell? What was that about?"

Dean looked at his phone, not caring about the road, even though cars beeped their horns and drove around him. "I got a text from the doctor. He's running behind."

"So...." Jonesy questioned. "Come on, let's go. Before we get pulled over."

"On account of the doctor running late, I'm gonna make a pitstop."

"Woah! Woah! There's no time brother Dean. We need to get there ASAP, regardless." Reno said.

"Yeah you fucktard! Do you want me to beat you over the head with the nineiron in the trunk?" Jonesy said.

Dean was young, thin, buzz cut hair with piercings all over his face. He had on shades too but flipped them up and turned around to look at the three men sitting in the backseat, Sir Penn in the middle, Jonesy and Reno next to him. They immediately noticed his puffy eyes and constricted pupils. They knew the deal.

"Dean! You told us you were off the *grisly*. Haven't you been sober for eighteen months?"

"Yeah but I'm dying for a hit." Dean said. "I'll give you both a cut of my dough after we split it. As long as you don't mention this to the doctor. No matter what. Capeesh?" Reno and Jonesy looked at each other in the backseat. "Please!" Dean pleaded.

"Better make this the fastest deal of your life. We can't afford a slip up." Reno said.

"Don't worry. The doctor told me Sir Penn will be sleeping in the Hudson River soon. Right beside his dear friend Xavier Bonaparte, the famous lawyer." They all laughed as Dean drove the van on Lafayette street and a quick right onto Market Street. "Dean, tell me you're not stopping on Market Street? There's too many people here. You'd be an idiot."

"No way. But look. Do you see that guy on the corner.." He pointed through the tinted window at a seven foot tall man with massive hands. "That's Shoemaker. He's the premier drug dealer in Brick City, but he only sells fake stuff to the out of towners. Believe me I know."

"Ohh yeah?" Reno asked, not really caring.

"Yeah, Shoemaker burned me a couple times too back in the day," Jonesy replied. "So where are you going then?"

"I'm meeting Eli. He's always reliable."

"I heard Eli's been living at the train station." Jonesy said.

"Yeah he was for a little bit. But he's got a pad now. He lives with some old guy who says he's Anthony Hopkins, the actor, kinda looks like him too."

"It's not really him though, is it?" Reno inquired.

"I'm not sure, but everyone in the neighborhood says it is. He's a quiet old man, sits at home and watches Judge Judy. If he ever needs to leave it's always in an all black tinted limo. Maybe it is him.. Who knows?" Dean shrugged his shoulders, stopped at a stop sign and looked both ways. "But Eli's in the basement apartment getting the business back on track." Dean rambled on.

"Good for him." Reno said, but he and Jonesy were losing interest so they took out their phones and checked their social media feeds. All the posts were either about Guns, Women, and/or Golf. Reno gawked at a picture of a woman in a bikini and pistol at her hip.

"All she needs is a good stroke game."

"When's Ginny coming back to the Village Green? She's the hottest chick I've ever seen hold a put."

"I don't know. But let's make sure we're there, I could watch her swing all day long."

The van turned down Lily Lane, a narrow one way side street. Dean double parked in the middle of the road and picked up his phone. "Yeah I'm outside. Give me a full setup." Then he hung up, exited the vehicle and ran up to the house.

"I swear Reno, if Dean F's this up, you're taking full responsibility."

"What! If this is anyone's fault it's yours. You cleared his name so he could take this job."

"Yeah but I have kids and it's tough to raise little ones on the streets." Jonesy said. "And what do you have? A crazy ex-girlfriend who won't leave you alone. You're taking the blame."

"I won't take the blame! And leave Shania out of this!" A couple minutes go by, and their van is still idling in the middle of the road.

Jonesy noticed a few shadows walking through the windows of the house, as well as a long stretch of cats gathering underneath the front porch searching for food. "Come on Dean! Hurry your ass up!"

II

Then a car pulled up behind the van on the one way street and beeped its horn.

Beep! Beep! BEEP!!

"Get off the road!" An elderly woman stuck her head out her car window.

"Damn it Dean!" Jonesy said.

Then the front door of the house opened and Dean ran frantically down the porch steps. But before he could make it to the sidewalk, a shadow appeared in the door frame and shot Dean twice in the back. He fell down the last few steps and blood spewed from his body onto the concrete.

"Holy fuck! Fuck! Reno! Drive!"

Reno jumped into the driver's seat and sped off wildly, sideswiping a couple parked cars. The man from the house shot bullets at the van, and one went right through the back window, grazing Sir Penn's head; it blew through the upholstery of the passenger seat and out the passenger window. Glass shattered everywhere. Reno turned off Lily Lane and regained his composure.

"Who the hell was that? That wasn't Eli, was it?"

"I've never seen that man before. Fuck! FUCK! The shit this kid got us into!" Jonesy screamed at the top of his lungs.

"You're gonna have to answer the doctor on this one. But look at the bright side… One less person to split the spoils with." Reno said. "Should we call Gloves?"

"Yeah let's tell him we're on our way… But hey! Wait a second." Jonesy thought, scratching his chin. "What's our story? Cause I'm not missing out on payday because of a dumb ass kid!"

III

At the testing facility, Reno and Jonesy waited for the doctor to arrive, corroborating on their story but it felt like no use. "He'll know we're lying." Reno said. "Maybe the truth will spare us."

They bickered back and forth for twenty-five minutes until they heard the sound of the back door open and the doctor walked in.

"After seeing the state of that van outside, I must say I am not the least surprised." The doctor said, shaking his head.

"It was the kid's fault!" Reno blurted out. "He stopped to get a bag of the *grisly* and we barely escaped alive."

"Damn it! Didn't I give you orders not to stop anywhere under any circumstances?" The doctor cringed. "Did anyone notice Sir Penn in the car?"

"I don't think so." Jonesy said.

"So where's Dean now?" The doctor asked.

"He's dead." Reno said coldly.

"I had a bad feeling about you three! This mission was already fragile enough! God forbid I have one more stupid henchmen on my side. I'd like to see you all suffer. And you especially Jonesy! You've been on my shit list for a long time, so here's your reward. I'll have Gloves glue your balls to the cement, then you'll starve and eat your own vomit." Jonesy stared bewildered at the doctor's speech.

"Don't worry Reno! I need you… mainly for my experiments," The doctor said. "In the next room I have a drug that will bring me millions, possibly billions of dollars in profit. So rest assured Reno, all will be well. You may find that this medication makes you stronger, faster and more agile than ever."

"I trust you doc!" Reno said.

"I'll be back, but there's something I must take care of first" The doctor exited the room and walked down the hall to room **A13**, the main examining room where Sir Penn was restrained. The doctor looked through the glass and was shocked to see Sir Penn sitting up awake, with his legs dangling over the edge of the examining table. "Gloves get down here!"

Gloves ran down the steps. "Yes doc."

"I told you to sedate him! He should have been shot up with the morphine." He pointed at Sir Penn through the see-through glass.

"I gave him twelve doses like you said."

"It was supposed to be thirteen."

"I would have but after the twelfth dose, his feet kicked out and for a second I thought he was dead. I didn't want to chance it."

"Well you should have chanced it. Nevermind now. Go upstairs, watch the cameras and wait for Sordenburg. I must be undisturbed until my experiments are complete. Understood?" He looked at Gloves, disappointed then turned to the door of **A13**. "Now please excuse me." He entered the room to greet Sir Penn. The air was thick.

Sir Penn heard the door and sat motionless like a possum with his hands and legs shackled. The doctor grabbed a syringe from his desk, turned to the center of the room and jumped in fright upon seeing Sir

Penn with his head turned 360 degrees staring wide-eyed. "Good to see you again Doc. How long's it been since my last visit?"

"Ah you devil, you've been a pain in my ass since Day One. You know how to dip and dodge your way out of tight situations, but listen Penn! I've got you trapped in my lab and nobody is coming to release you!"

"So you think you'll slam and jam your way to a multi-billion dollar enterprise. You're ludicrous!"

"If Mr. Frazier can muscle his way to be one of the top ten richest in the country, then I can too." The doctor grabbed a test beaker with his back turned to Sir Penn. "But Frazier sold overpriced diamonds because he made a deal with the Russians. He got a lucky break. I, on the other hand, have worked hard for my reward!"

"My strength will not fail me. No matter what you do to me."

"Ha! Funny boy! Guess I'll just have to give you the sleeping gas to shut you up, since the morphine wouldn't cut it." Dr. Trevis went over to his desk and typed in a command on a computer tablet screen. "Don't worry this will be over before you know it." He pressed a button on the tablet and the tablet responded, "releasing toxic gas in 15 seconds."

"15… 14… 13… 12…" The doctor walked nonchalantly to the door. "Any last words you'd like to say Sir Penn?"

"10…9…8…" Sir Penn shook his head, but prayed under his breath. *"God, please guide me and protect me so that I may finish what I was brought here on Earth for."*

The doctor exited the room before it started to fill up with sleeping gas. Sir Penn was unconscious in a few seconds.

IV

Sir Penn stood in a dimly lit hallway. The floor covered in dirt. He saw doors on his left and right as far as his eye could see, but all the doors were boarded up. "Jesus!" He looked around in disbelief, noticing broken end tables and decorative lamps destroyed on the floor. He moved forward, looking for a door that wasn't boarded.

A gargantuan loud noise occurred behind him. Boom! BOOM! It sounded like an earthquake. He looked behind him and saw nothing but darkness behind him down the corridor. Then a foreboding voice said. "Well, well, well Sir Penn. I have you just where I want you."

"Who is that?" He looked around, shifting his focus through the darkness, seeing nothing.

"Just wait and see." The voice was coming closer. Sir Penn sprinted in the opposite direction. He could hear ominous footsteps following closely behind him. He hurdled over debris, shards of glass, old paintings, and a few gaping sized holes in the floor. The footsteps gained on him, so Sir Penn picked up his speed, hoping he didn't run out of stamina. "Come on!" He said under his breath. "I must pick up the pace." He sprinted. Then yelled, "What the fuck!" Noticing every door still boarded up. Then, there, he saw a door on his right which didn't have any boards covering it. He wrestled the knob and now saw a large brute of a man approaching him, sliding a sledgehammer along the floor. The brute's head was oblong, his cheeks were plump, and his arms were lanky. He was twenty yards away. The brute said, "Stop right there Penn. You are mine!" Sir Penn tugged again at the doorknob, feeling the creature coming closer. He could almost smell the monster's breath. "You can't run anymore. I've got you." The creature gripped Sir Penn's shoulder but Penn shook him off and dove directly through the entryway, leaving a hole in the wood door.

...

Sir Penn had his back on the ground up against the Elizabeth train tracks as a train whistled in the distance. The monster from the hallway was now on the platform above, wearing a long trench coat and staring down at him. The monster's oblong face had an ear to ear grin, as he opened his trench coat and revealed an assortment of weapons: axes, guns, swords, nunchucks, baseball bats, and a chainsaw. "What's all that for?" Penn yelled up to him as the brute closed his trenchcoat.

"You'll see. Now take me to where I want to go." The monster said.

Upon hearing these words, Sir Penn felt compelled to get up from the train tracks and start walking towards Alistor Street. "Who are you?" Penn asked the monster who was following him closely behind.

"You'll see." The creature replied in a hoarse voice.

Penn turned down a side street where every house on both sides of the road looked identical, gray and gloomy. He crossed many streets like this until realizing that the upcoming street was different. For one thing, these houses weren't gray, instead they were vibrant with manicured lawns, colorful flowers and evergreen trees in front of them. There were even dogs running on the street, barking playfully together.

Penn continued walking, smiling, enjoying the calm feeling this street gave him, until he stopped compulsively in front of a dark green house with black shutters. It was a two story house with concrete steps leading up to a wraparound porch. All it needed was a paint job. Penn stopped in awe, reminded of his childhood home on Alistor Street. *If there was an exact replica this would be it,* he thought.

"Well… Go on." The brute said, with a grin showing his teeth.

"Why don't you go first?" Penn asked. "This is obviously the right place."

"Because this is your story and you are paving the way."

Penn walked up to the front door, trying with all of his strength to stop the compulsion. But the more he resisted the more his body hurt. He fell down and crawled towards the porch steps. "Get up!" The brute screamed.

Penn got up slowly and ascended the last couple steps leading to a light brown front door, where a note said: 'ONLY YOU CAN OPEN THE DOOR SIR PENN. THE KEY IS IN YOUR POCKET.' Penn fumbled in his pants pocket and found an old rusted skeleton key. He put the key into the padlock as the creature breathed down his neck. Penn unlocked the door and immediately felt nostalgic upon entering. An aroma of garlic and onions with a hint of rosemary came from the kitchen. And all the furnishings were in the same position he remembered from his childhood home. The dining room light was even on like it always was.

He looked down at his foot planted on a welcome mat with a picture of New Jersey on it. And behind him, the brute was outside with his oblong face pressed against the screen door. "Invite me in." Penn held back from opening the screen door out of sheer willpower, but after a minute, he felt his arm about to break. "You must let me in NOW!" The brute said, banging on the screen until Penn couldn't withstand the pain anymore, opened the screen door and said, "You may enter."

"Brghhhhh." The man barrelled forth, leveling Sir Penn to the ground. Then he pulled out a chainsaw from his trenchcoat and cut into the sheetrock walls.

Penn rolled over and pushed himself up. He had no idea what the implications were, but he knew this intruder was creating a profound effect on his life. Dream or no dream, this was real. "What are you doing?" Penn screamed over the sound of the chainsaw as water gushed from cut pipes in the wall.

"Something that should have been done a long time ago. I am tearing up your security and leaving you with nothing. The fortress you have built will be no more, and then I will have the secrets to your past success."

"You're mad! You are just a projection of fear from my subconscious mind!" The monster dropped the saw and left sheetrock all over the floor, as pipes continued spewing water and sewage everywhere. The stench became horrible. Then the monster took out a Louisvill bat from his trenchcoat and swung it into Sir Penn's chest, knocking him back.

"Now don't get it twisted Sir Penn." It said, stammering the bat against the floor. "I am the only tangible thing you have left, and I am much stronger than you could ever imagine. You thought you released your fears but they have come back to haunt you," He snickered, then smashed the bat into Sir Penn's stomach, cracking two of his ribs. "Your fear is right here, tearing apart your preconceived notions." The brute left Sir Penn on the ground and continued wrecking the house.

After a few minutes, Penn rolled over and mustered up the courage to run. He jetted straight out of the house, feeling like each step would be his last. He tripped, clumsily, over a branch that had fallen in the yard. As he got up he heard the front door slam. The brute ran out, without his trenchcoat. His stomach looked like the face of 'the predator' and was covered in blood. Sir Penn picked himself up only to trip again a few yards later on an uneven sidewalk. It was hopeless. He didn't have any more energy so he knelt down, closed his eyes and prayed from the bottom of his heart.

…

The thumping of footsteps stopped. After a second of silence, he opened his eyes in an open field and saw a candle flickering in the breeze up ahead. Sir Penn got closer to the candle light and called out, "Who's there?"

"It's Xavier." I said, revealing my face from behind the flickering light. And there I stood face-to-face with Sir Penn.

"You're the last person I'd expect to see here." Sir Penn said.

"Oh yeah, why's that?" I asked.

"Because you stole millions of diamonds from Mr. Frazier and the Tri-Cities. Why would you dare show your face again?"

"If you only knew the amount of treachery I've been in," I said, as a light mist came from the sky. "Ill-begotten money is a death trap."

"Huh?" Sir Penn questioned. "You're the modern Robin Hood. Everybody knows Frazier deserved it."

"Mr. Frazier has made his money doing something none of us understand. Good or evil, he'll get his karma."

V

Rich stopped out of breath, seeing the gang of runaway workers crawl under a fence and disappear from sight, near the Cherry Street Bridge. The bridge crossed over the New Jersey reservoir, a circular body of water one hundred and forty feet wide, separating the Brick City from the Tri-Cities. The top of the bridge had been barricaded off by police so no one could cross into the Tri-Cities, and the police deposited flesh eating bacteria into the reservoir so no one could swim across. Even if anyone tried, they'd be devoured within minutes.

The moon was shining across the water gap and illuminated a small settlement under the bridge, on the edge of the reservoir. It was a small village that reeked of rotten sewage, where runaway teenagers and homeless people constructed tents from tree branches and donated towels (for insulation) they received from the local church.

Rich noticed the sewer grate near his foot had an aerial view of the settlement under the bridge. He got down on his stomach and looked in. He watched as three girls fought over a designer purse, all of them tugging at the strap.

"That's mine. Give it here!" A thin woman said. She was dressed in a yellow colored blouse, a white skirt and had her hair tied back.

"Tough luck. If you don't like it you can get on out of here!"

"Shania, cut it out! It's her first day here. Why are you roughing her up already?"

"Listen Caitlin, I gotta teach this new girl how to share if she wants to be one of us!" Shania, wearing a red colored blouse and torn up jeans was the tallest and strongest of the three. She now had the purse clutched in her hands. "You and your punk boyfriend need to pay your dues." She pushed the thin woman, who tripped over a stone and tumbled sideways, covering her white skirt in mud. Shania, meanwhile, looked in the purse and pulled out something shiny. A diamond.

"What the hell is this?" Shania said, examining it. "Is this real?"

"Don't touch that!" The woman on the ground yelled.

"Ohhhh or else what?" Shania flaunted.

"Let me see, I'll tell you if it's real." Caitlin snatched it and examined it. Caitlin wore an old brown dress with ruffles on the bottom below her knees. She had a nose piercing and a necklace with a pink stone on it. Her hair was slung down her side and reached just past her shoulders. She was in awe looking at the diamond and noticed its inscription, **A13**.

"It looks real. Where'd you get this?" Caitlin asked the woman on the ground.

"I found it somewhere."

"Don't give me that bullshit." Shania snatched the diamond back from Caitlin. "What'd you have to do for this? Strip? Cause I'll do that right here for another one." Shania said, partly serious.

"No. Of course not."

"You know I wouldn't mind if you did strip. Cause even with mud all over you, you're still a cutie. What's your name again?"

"Selah!"

"I know what we'll call you… sexy stripper Selah."

Selah grew furious and stepped up from the mud and stood directly in front of Shania, ready to fight. "I've had enough of this! That purse is mine and the diamond is mine!"

"If you make one more move like that Selah, I'll make sure you and your boyfriend get tossed into the reservoir." Shania spit on the diamond and wiped off a bit of dirt from it so it glistened. "This is mine now. Here you can have the stupid purse back, thank you." Shania threw Selah's purse into the mud, then put the diamond in her pocket and smiled. Shania never felt so rich in her life; but as soon as she was about to walk away, she froze in place.

"What's wrong Shania?" Caitlin asked. Shania was unresponsive, and her hands were trembling. "What'd you do to her!" Caitlin pushed Selah back into the mud.

Rich watched the three women fighting through the grating, and noticed the glistening of the diamond. At that moment a gang of fifteen teenagers, each with a crossbow sling on their backs, walked up behind him. The gang all wore a similar uniform, a ripped tank top, khaki shorts and black face paint on their face.

"Hey what are you doing? Spying you old fuck, get out of here!" They surrounded him. Rich stood up and put his hands up. "No. Nothing like that."

"This is our territory," the kid in the middle said with a crooked smile, extenuating his emaciated face. He pulled out a crossbow and aimed it at Rich from a foot away. The other teenagers followed suit and wielded their crossbows from their backs and the entire gang surrounded him. "If you're not out of here in five seconds we're gonna throw you into the reservoir. I think I hear the fish singing already."

"No, it's okay. I'm leaving now!" Rich, with his hands up, started to shimmy out of the circle when one of the teenagers kicked him in the nuts. "Damn! What was that for?" He asked, hopping up and down holding his crotch.

"Why were you tailing those women? I saw you running after them." The boy pulled Rich onto the floor. "Instead of letting you go. It'd be more fun to stuff your head and leave it on the front steps of the precinct."

"What… no… please." Rich cleared his throat. "I wanted to make sure they were safe. My friend and I helped them escape an illegal sweatshop this morning."

"You mean The Creep's enterprise? We've been trying to do that for months!" He said, putting his crossbow back in its sheath. Then everyone else followed suit, lowering their crossbows and putting them on their backs. "Sorry we doubted you. Those men came here one day and kidnapped about seventy young girls. But if they're inside the gate that means they're safe now. We've upgraded our weapons and all our defenses."

"Do you know who that girl is down there?" Rich pointed at Selah through the sewer grate. "What's she doing here?"

"What's that got to do with you?"

"Just trying to help you out looks like she's causing a commotion."

"Her and her friend came by last night." The boy in the middle said. "Her friend's over there." He pointed at a man standing a way's off in the dark, smoking a cigarette. "He likes to be alone. See him with a shaved head and baggy clothes?".

The clouds were getting darker and the air felt moist like a wet towel. It was about to rain. The Brick City streets never felt more foreboding.

VI

Rich walked away from the gang of teenagers, and headed towards me. I put out my cigarette and watched him move closer. "What's your business here?" I asked him from about ten feet away. Rich ignored my call and kept approaching. I pulled out my gun and pointed it at him, just as it started to rain.

"What's your business here?" I asked again. "If you wanna live you'd better turn around. Fast!"

Rich kept approaching and smiled. "Xavier, is that you?"

"Listen bud!" I said in a rough tone. "I'll give you a minute 'fore I blow your brains into shattered marbles."

"Xavier, I'm on your side. You gotta trust me." He moved even closer.

"Stay where you are. Don't tempt me. One wrong move and you're toast."

"You shouldn't be worried about me. Mr. Frazier is the one looking for you."

"I'm not scared of Frazier." I said.

"Apparently you're really testing your luck. You should have never come here. And why would you bring Selah too?"

I shook my head in shame.

"Quick car!" Rich shouted. And both of us crouched down as a Cadillac CTS sedan drove by slowly, its headlights shone past us for a split second. "Thank God, he didn't see us," Rich and I both got up, now with our shirts and pants soaked from the wet grass. However, as soon as we got up the same car pulled around and was heading back towards us again. This time the driver noticed us.

"Fuck he saw us!" I yelled. "It's gotta be Alin, I know Frazier sent him."

"What should we do?" Rich asked, seeing the car approach.

"I have to get Selah out of here." I replied. "I don't care about myself, as long as she's safe."

"Where are the diamonds?" Rich asked me.

"I got 'em stashed. I was supposed to be meeting Donald Eddy near here, but I don't care about the money. I only care about her. I'll trade all the diamonds for her. Rich, you have to do something for me."

"I'm listening." He said.

I told Rich where I hid the diamonds, and that they were his as long as he did me one favor. He agreed. I couldn't care less about the diamonds at this point. I just had to keep Selah safe.

I ran across the paved street. The nearest streetlamp was out so I slid between two parked cars and then waited because that suspicious car stopped in the middle of the road. The entrance to the settlement was just up ahead and I had to get there and find Selah.

The rain was coming down harder, and a fog swept the area making it difficult to see. I ran for it, across the road, and slipped on the wet pavement, dropping my gun down the metal grating into the settlement under the Cherry Street Bridge. Then I lunged underneath the fence to find Selah.

Rich shuffled behind a bush, as someone stepped out from the car. "Come out X! We know you're back there!"

The man beamed a flashlight in Rich's direction. The rain was intensifying.

In a split moment, Rich came running out from behind his bush and tackled the man with the flashlight, punched him in the face twice and knocked him out. Rich stole the man's firearm. Visibility was getting worse. Two more men stepped out of the car, "Hey what's going on over there?"

Rich slid back into the shrubbery clutching his newfound gun. He watched the small shadowy figures approaching in the distance.

Rich fired four bullets, blindly into the night, and almost hit one man in the leg. The chamber was almost empty. He had two bullets left, but he wanted to save them for the mission that I had given him. He remained hidden while I resurfaced from the settlement with my gun in hand and Selah behind me. I shot towards the car and the two men.

"Xavier, we have you cornered. Don't make this difficult."

"Good luck!" I screamed, reloading my gun and hiding with Selah behind a parked car on the side of the road.

"We're calling for backup X! Now's your last chance to come out."

"Selah you need to run! Just get out of here, it's dangerous." I turned to her and said.

"No, I'm staying."

"Wherever you go I'll find you." I said. We kissed passionately as bullets were fired our way.

"I'm not leaving!" She said adamantly. I never loved her more.

I leaned out and shot two more times towards the car in the distance, this time I hit one of the men in the chest. I watched as the man staggered, but then continued walking towards us. I knew Frazier wouldn't send his men out without bulletproof vests. I crouched back next to her. "You're in danger, Selah. Now's your chance to escape. I'll cover you."

"We're in this together babe." She replied.

"Hey Alin! Grab the rocket launcher." I heard one of the men say down the street. Then Alin grabbed a rocket launcher from the car trunk and began loading it.

"Run!" Rich screamed from across the street. Selah and I ran away just in time as Alin let off a rocket that caused three parked cars near us to explode on impact. Shards of debris flew into the road.

Selah and I crouched down and shielded one another in our arms. I could barely see anything beyond the fire bellowing but I still had to fight for her. I stood up and shot blindly into the blaze. Then another gun fired in our direction. The shots whizzed by our heads. Then silence. The bullets ceased for a minute. I looked out from my position and saw two dark shadows approaching.

"Come out Xavier!"

I tried to shoot again but I was out of ammo.

"Fuck!" I banged the gun on the side of another parked car. Visibility was horrible; the whole area looked like a war scene. Rich remained hidden behind the shrubbery across the street. "Rich get out of here. Make sure you do what I told you!" I yelled out to him.

Then I heard something flying in the air, and clink on the ground.

It was a grenade! A sleeping gas grenade.

The next thing I remember is that both Selah and I got lightheaded really fast.

"Put them both in the truck quickly!" Alin shouted. "And there's another guy across the street. Look beyond the landscaping."

Rich was already on the move, out to complete the mission I had given him. He was determined to do it even if it was the last thing he ever did. Or so he hoped.

"Alin, let's get out of here! It's the feds." Police sirens were approaching the vicinity.

Alin got in the driver's seat. The other accomplices threw Selah and myself inside the back trunk before they themselves hopped in the backseat. Alin sped off but two Brick City cop vehicles were now following behind him.

"Wait Alin! We got Xavier but what about the diamonds? We gotta go back." Ghost said.

"That's the least of our concerns right now. We have at least ten cop cars on our tail. The boss asked for Xavier. And since the girl is involved in this mess she comes too."

"What about the other guy who was across the street? He beat me up and stole my gun."

"In my eyes we got what we wanted. Now shut up and let me drive, no more questions Ghost."

Alin's phone rang. The words BOSS came up in bold letters on the car video monitor. "Great timing. Wonder what he wants."

"Tell him we expect to be paid tonight!"

"Shut up Dexter! Or the boss will treat you like he did Sparky yesterday," Alin said before answering the call: "Hey boss! How's it going?" The police sirens were loud in the background.

"What's going on Alin! What's all the commotion?"

"Well good news we picked up Xavier. But the bad news is we got a gang of cops tailing us right now.

"Fuck! Tell me you can lose them Alin."

"Of course boss! You don't call me Ace for nothing."

"Call me back when you've lost them." Mr. Frazier hung up.

"Dammit Alin! All I wanted to know is when are we gonna get paid?"

"I told you to shut your mouth, didn't I Dexter?"

Alin ruminated, feeling the thrill of the mission: *Everyone knew if you crossed Mr. Frazier you'd be found dead. Just look at Mr. Locklard, CEO of Lucky's who tried giving up Frazier to the police. He got what he deserved, a cold nitrogen blast tube fed into his ass. A slow viscous death. I'm sure Locklard would've loved another round of talks with the police. It's funny when you know there's only one thing you gotta do and you don't do it. Thank God I'm Frazier's number two. And I need that bonus! Oh I love this job.*

"Hold up Alin!" Ghost said. "There's a roadblock up ahead. Turn down the next street."

Alin slammed on the brakes now seeing the inconspicuous roadblock up ahead. "Thanks!" He turned down the next street, Lily Lane.

VII

Dexter and Ghost looked out the window at the narrow one way street, Lily Lane.

"I think we lost them Alin." Dexter said, noticing no cops behind them.

"Let's not count our blessings yet." Alin said.

"Wait, isn't this the street where that famous actor lives under the radar?"

"Who's that?"

"Anthony Hopkins. The actor who played that famous serial killer."

"Yeah right! Fuck off!"

"For real, I wouldn't pull your leg. I've been over to Hopkin's place before. I did him a favor once." They all laugh. "I'm telling you, I could knock on the house at any time of the day. He'd be happy to see me."

Alin drove the Cadillac sedan onto the sidewalk to avoid hitting massive potholes. "Point the house to me." Alin said. "I want to see it. I might actually have some respect for you if it's true." Ghost pointed out to a small green shotgun house near the corner of the next intersection before Market Street.

"This one. Right here! And he's home too cause I see a light on in the basement."

"No way." Alin looked in disbelief. He couldn't imagine Hopkins living in such a tiny house.

Alin slowed down upon seeing a man from the house open the front door and step out onto the porch. The man was tall, brawny and dark skinned with a baggy shirt and a backwards hat. The guys inside the car looked and laughed amongst themselves.

"Obviously not Hopkins. I told you. You don't know what you're talking about."

"Hey wait…" Dexter said. "Isn't that Eli? That guy is bad news. We should leave."

Alin started sweating, he had fucked up, going down this road, and forgetting Xavier was the most important mission right now. Alin thought about his track record with Mr. Frazier. How he never fucked up a mission in ten years. He was the Ace! And he was about to fail the most important mission in his career? His heart sank. It was two minutes to midnight. They watched as Eli pulled out a semi automatic handgun behind his back.

Alin put his foot on the gas pedal and went to drive but was blocked in by twenty police cars. He went to back up in reverse and twenty more police cars blocked the road behind him. Alin stared out the rearview and trembled.

"Yo Alin get us out of here," Dexter said. Alin was frozen in indecision. "Times up Alin, come on. I can't afford another run in Rikers Island. I'd rather be in a mental asylum than back there."

"Shut up, let me think." Alin said under his breath.

The neighbors of the surrounding houses all came outside to observe the situation unfolding. Ten cops got out of their vehicles and approached Alin's car in the middle of the road."

"Everyone get out of the car with your hands up." The cops shouted.

BANG! BANG!

Alin turned his head hearing the sound of gunfire coming from the green house. It was Eli shooting at the cops. One bullet hit an officer right in the head, splattering his brains on the front windshield of Mr. Frazier's Cadillac.

"Holy fuck!" Alin ducked as another bullet whizzed by and hit the window but ricocheted off. *Thank God Frazier keeps everything bulletproof,* Alin thought.

Alin called Mr. Frazier, putting the phone on speaker. Mr. Frazier answered after the first ring.

"Please tell me you're all safe."

"No boss… and it's all my fault… I fucked-up."

"Fucked-up! Fucked-up!" Mr. Frazier's tone rose exponentially. "Alin you're flawless, please tell me this is a joke?"

"It's true boss. We're trapped on Lily Lane. The cops have blocked us from all directions and there's a shootout going on between a gang member and the cops. Oh shit! More cops are pulling in as we speak."

Mr. Frazier inhaled a long deep breath. "Alin… if I ever see you again wait til you see what I'm gonna do with you!"

There were fifty cops in the vicinity now shooting at the man on the porch of the green house. Eli was in a prone position firing his semi automatic as cops inched closer and surrounded the porch of the house. Then in a split second, Eli disappeared and a few cops walked up to the front door and were about to kick it open when...

BOOOOOOOOOMMMMMM!!!

A huge bomb went off near the front door, blowing up the entire porch. Bodies flew everywhere and Alin's car shook from the shock.

"What the hell's going on Alin?" Frazier asked, still on the other line. Alin was in terror looking at the scene.

"It's a frenzy over here. But I think I can get away amidst this mess."

The cops were preoccupied, all of them watched the house and shot into the rubble. Then more gunfire came from the house shooting at cops that were still alive.

In the chaos, Alin revved the engine and drove between two police cars, barreling his way through. The bumper of the Cadillac fell off but he continued on, turning right onto Market Street.

"Don't worry boss, I somehow got a second chance."

Alin looked into the rearview and saw two cop cars now following him. "Shit I got two cops on my tail."

"You better drive. Perhaps you can still get that bonus.". Frazier conceded. "All I need is Xavier in one piece."

Alin sped down Market. The two cop cars behind him kept up with him neck and neck. Alin braked hard and made a quick left. But the cops were still right behind him. Alin turned to go down another side street, but he misjudged the turn and hit a high curb at an awkward angle. The entire car flipped over multiple times on the road.

…

Detective Dick Sordenburg, dressed in a black suit and tie, got out of the squad car followed by four police officers. He relayed the orders, "Get Xavier and Selah out of the trunk and bring them to the doctors lab. Hurry before the news media gets here!" Detective Sordenburg picked up his phone to call Dr. Trevis, "they'll be on their way," was all he said then hung up.

The officers struggled to open the trunk of the overturned Cadillac.

The detective barked his orders again, "Come on, grab them and let's go!"

VIII

The four policemen ran inside the doctor's lab, carrying Selah and me. The policeman entered a small vestibule with a round table leading to a long hallway on the other end.

Gloves sat at the table and greeted them with a face of disbelief. "Why so late?"

"Where do we put the body?" The lanky officer with the large nose asked.

"In the basement. Put Xavier and Selah in room number 12 on top of the two lab tables. The doctor has been waiting."

The policemen went down the steps with the bodies and walked up to room 12. Dr. Trevis was already there and watched as the officers placed us on the lab tables.

"Perfect. Thank you officers," Dr. Trevis said.

"The detective is on his way down here, he wants to renegotiate the terms of the agreement."

"There's no time for that. I'm in the final stages of my research." Dr. Trevis pulled out a long needle from his pocket and pointed it at the officers. The cops began walking out of the room, "Tell him we'll all be in the Cayman Islands soon!"

I was lying down on the table when the doctor approached me, sticking a needle into my brain and extracting my subconscious fluid. "There. There." He completely filled a small vial with fluid. "I almost have everything I need." Dr. Trevis took the vial of fluid and placed it into a CPR centrifuge. The timer lit up, counting down from 90 seconds, then the machine shook violently. While waiting, the doctor took out his phone to call Gloves.

"It's nearly ready. Bring Jonesy and Reno in here as my extra test subjects!"

The centrifuge beeped indicating that the mixture was complete. Dr. Trevis took out the vial and stared at the fluid. Then he heard a commotion in the hallway and opened the door and saw Gloves pinned to the wall by Jonesy.

"You ignoramus!" Jonesy said, pelting Gloves in the stomach and groin. "You believe the doctor is gonna let you live!" Gloves stopped moving because he had a broken rib that punctured his lung, giving him traumatic pneumothorax. Dr. Trevis closed the door of the lab and called the detective.

"We have a situation in the basement. Send your men down to handle it."

"Not until we renegotiate our terms."

"For Christ's sake detective, you know we're in this together! Get your men down here. Now!"

Dr. Trevis hung up the phone and now Jonesy was charging at the door. Jonesy barrelled into the door and shook the doorframe. Dr. Trevis blocked the entrance with a trolley cart of medical supplies.

"Dammit!" Dr. Trevis yelped, taking the subconscious fluid from Xavier and mixing it with Sir Penn's subconscious fluid. The mixture swirled like a cloudy membrane until settling into a gray thick paste. He stared in wonder at the permanence. "'Tis done!" He held up the vial to the light.

Now Reno appeared next to Jonesy and they both charged the door, this time breaking it off its hinges.

"Stay back!" The doctor screamed at them.

"Say your prayers Doc. This will be the last experiment you ever do!"

"Jonesy, Reno, please, you must understand." The doctor backed away slowly and showed them the vial. "This is going to be worth billions."

Detective Sordenburg appeared in the door frame with a pistol drawn and shot the doctor in the stomach. "Thanks for your service doctor." The doctor dropped the vial, which clinked onto the floor but didn't crack. "And you two on the ground!" The detective said, addressing Jonesy and Reno.

The doctor had blood spraying out from his chest, but still managed to reach the vial on the floor. He took an empty syringe from his coat pocket and filled it with the fluid from the vial. "It didn't have to be this way." The doctor said, injecting himself in the head with the fluid. But before he could finish injecting the entire syringe, Detective Sordenburg shot the doctor three more times in the stomach. The doctor flopped over, appearing to be dead.

"Ahhh this is a big moment." Detective Sordenburg walked over and took the syringe out of the doctor's head. "There's still a little fluid left" He said leaving the doctor on the ground, helpless.

"You may be exempt from all charges if you cooperate with the Tri-City government." The detective said to Jonesy and Reno.

"Never! I'm not a rat! I'd rather go back to prison." Jonesy said.

Then out of the corner of their eyes they saw the doctor moving again. "What the fuck!" The detective shot the doctor two more times, then reloaded his gun.

"Detective!" Said a voice in the hall. It was a policeman with an assault rifle in his arms. The detective walked over to the door. Joncsy and Reno attempted to stand up and follow him. "Stay back!" The officer in the doorway said, pointing his gun at them. The detective crossed the threshold, and stood in the hallway.

"We have what we need, Alvarez. This is going to be the discovery of the century!" The detective said in the hallway.

"There's an unmarked car waiting to squeeze us out of here." Alvarez said.

"No, we need to play this safe. And we can't afford any suspicion."

…

Dr. Trevis began foaming from the mouth and his face changed into a horrible rectangular shape. He stood up, reached into his white coat that looked like bloody Swiss cheese with bullet holes in it, and took out a loaded syringe from his pocket. He fumbled over to Selah, who was lying on the lab table next to me and injected her in the head with the syringe.

The doctor took the syringe out of Selah's head and injected the remaining fluid into my neck.

"Doctor! What the fuck!" Jonesy and Reno screamed.

"Is this really happening?" Reno trembled, staring in bewilderment as the doctor took out another syringe from his pocket and walked up to them. "Jonesy. Reno. This will all be over soon."

Jonesy ran from his position and tackled the doctor to the ground. Then he sunk his fingers into the doctor's eyes like a bowling ball to gouge them out, while Reno grabbed a surgeon's knife from the desk and stabbed the doctor in the chest.

The doctor wasn't affected at all by their attacks, in fact, it just made him angry. He pushed Jonesy and Reno so hard they flew across the room and hit the back wall. The doctor jumped forward, right in front of Jonesy and ripped both his legs off. "You motherfuc….." Jonesy tried to say, before his legs detached from his body.

The doctor looked at Reno, then ripped out Reno's heart and shoved it in his mouth, licking his lips like it was a treat.

Detective Sordenburg and Officer Alvarez, hearing the commotion, peeked into the room and ran out the building frantically upon seeing Dr. Trevis tear out Reno's heart and eat it.

Dr. Trevis, still with blood oozing out of his gunshot wounds, crawled towards the centrifuge, took out a new syringe and stumbled into the hallway over to the next room where Sir Penn lay unconscious. He opened the door, toxic gas that he let off previously had now dispelled. He was about to stick the needle into Sir Penn's head but before he could he became dizzy and fell over. Dr. Trevis regained his strength a second later and held onto the countertop sink.

The doctor looked up and saw Sir Penn, awake, creeping up towards him. "It will never work because you don't have the antidote," Sir Penn said, grabbing the doctor's coat, attempting to pull him down. But the doctor turned and chucked Sir Penn across the room effortlessly. Most of the bones in Sir Penn's body broke upon impact on the stone wall. "Stop! Help! Help!" Sir Penn supplicated.

Dr. Trevis picked up Sir Penn's fragile body and snapped him in half right at the torso, leaving his arms and chest on one side of the room and his legs and pelvis on the other side. But Sir Penn's arms were still moving, and he was inching his upper body toward a long mirror in the corner of the room, leaving behind a blood stain trail. Sir Penn held out his arm to touch the mirror and as soon as he did, he got sucked in.

Dr. Trevis looked at the mirror in the corner of the room and saw a young man in a suit and tie staring back at him. The man in the mirror stuck out his finger and beckoned the doctor to approach. The doctor crawled forward and when he reached the mirror he was sucked in next.

...

Selah woke up. She saw me lying unconscious on the lab table beside her. She kissed me. "Babe! Wake up! It's all over." She sobbed, her tears dripped onto my cheek. "Please. Wake up!"

I woke up, staring into Selah's eyes. We began to embrace naturally, our faces wearing away by the second into skin and bone (a side effect of the medication the doctor gave us). But we kissed passionately even as blood dripped from our lips.

Our bodies, together in deathly matrimony, drowning out the senses of the world around us; we stared into each other's eyes and smiled at one another. We kissed one last time. Tears fell majestically from our faces and I held her tight. I was entranced by her as I had always been. "Close your eyes," I told her. "It'll all be better."

…

A crowd of spectators began to form on the street where the doctor's lab was. "You sure the lab is cleared." Detective Sordenburg asked a group of policemen.

"No sign of Sir Penn or Dr. Trevis," the cop with the large nose said under his breath. "We've checked the place four times."

Suddenly, there was a strong gust of wind that sent a chill down Detective Sordenburg's spine as he stared at the scene. Medical personnel were running inside the building frantically.

"Everything alright detective?" Another cop asked him.

"Yes." He patted his breast pocket to make sure the vial was still there. "Soon we'll have access to this global weapon."

Helicopters surrounded overhead and news vans parked just beyond the police barricades, pointing their cameras at the scene.

"But what about the stolen diamonds?" Officer Alvarez asked him.

"All in good time. I know where they are," Sordenburg said, taking out his phone and dialing the Frazier residence. The phone rang once before someone picked up.

Epilogue

Rich found the duffle bag. I told him where I hid it and that it was all his as long as he could do one thing. The one thing which I believed would dispel the curse of the diamonds. He needed to break into Mr. Frazier's compound on Alistor Street and kill Frazier in cold blood.

Rich broke the pin pad of the rustic gate, which led to Frazier's mansion. The gate opened just enough so Rich could squeeze through. He ascended down the driveway into the courtyard and up to the massive cathedral doors, and pushed them open. He switched the duffle bag to his left side because the strap was beginning to dig into his shoulder.

"Anyone home?" He called out, loud enough so his voice echoed in the house. The place felt empty. He walked over to the parlor room in the back. No one. He went into the kitchen. No one. He looked outside the window into the yard. There was no movement on the patio or even on the lawn. No sign of anyone downstairs so he lugged the bag up the spiral staircase, holding onto the majestic pearl banister, and admiring the immaculate chandelier in the center.

Once on the landing he yelled, "Frazier!" a couple times but still no response. While upstairs he noticed every door open, except one. He walked up to the closed door and pushed it open. It was the master bedroom, and there Frazier laid face up on the bed with his eyes closed. He was alive because Rich could see his chest moving up and down. No noise was ever able to disturb Fraizer when he was in a deep sleep.

Rich put the duffle bag down and opened the top pouch. Sitting there on top of the diamonds was a .45 Desert Eagle, with two bullets left. He took it out and put the cold barrel up to Frazier's forehead. Frazier's eyes popped open in terror.

Rich shot twice and blasted Frazier's head to a pulp. The shots echoed through the house.

Then the phone rang on the bedside table.

"Hello," Rich answered.

"Who is this?" The man on the phone said. "Where's Mr. Frazier?"

"The diamonds made me do it. The diamonds made me do it." Rich trembled at the receiver.